SPLIT DECISION

"You boys better make up your minds," Clint said. "Leave, or make a move."

The two men realized that in order to leave they would have to go by Clint Adams. Both of them, knowing the reputation of the Gunsmith as a gunman and a killer, could not imagine that he would let them go so easily.

"You'd kill us if we tried to leave," Lee said. "We got no choice here, Adams."

"I'm giving you a choice," Clint said. "Live or die. Doesn't sound like a hard decision to me."

"No choice," Lee said to his partner.

"I know."

Clint could see that the two men were going to make a move. They felt they had no other choice.

"Billy," he said, "get on the ground . . . now!"

Clint brought his gun up and shot both of them through the chest. They staggered back, bounced off each other, and crumpled to the ground.

DON'T MISS THESE
ALL-ACTION WESTERN SERIES
FROM THE BERKLEY PUBLISHING GROUP

THE GUNSMITH by J. R. Roberts

Clint Adams was a legend among lawmen, outlaws, and ladies. They called him . . . the Gunsmith.

LONGARM by Tabor Evans

The popular long-running series about Deputy U.S. Marshal Long—his life, his loves, his fight for justice.

SLOCUM by Jake Logan

Today's longest-running action Western. John Slocum rides a deadly trail of hot blood and cold steel.

BUSHWHACKERS by B. J. Lanagan

An action-packed series by the creators of Longarm! The rousing adventures of the most brutal gang of cutthroats ever assembled—Quantrill's Raiders.

DIAMONDBACK by Guy Brewer

Dex Yancey is Diamondback, a Southern gentleman turned con man when his brother cheats him out of the family fortune. Ladies love him. Gamblers hate him. But nobody pulls one over on Dex. . . .

WILDGUN by Jack Hanson

The blazing adventures of mountain man Will Barlow—from the creators of Longarm!

TEXAS TRACKER by Tom Calhoun

Meet J. T. Law: the most relentless—and dangerous—manhunter in all Texas. Where sheriffs and posses fail, he's the best man to bring in the most vicious outlaws—for a price.

THE GUNSMITH

THE MARSHAL OF KINGDOM

J. R. ROBERTS

JOVE BOOKS, NEW YORK

THE MARSHAL OF KINGDOM

A Jove Book / published by arrangement with
the author

PRINTING HISTORY
Jove edition / December 2002

Copyright © 2002 by Robert J. Randisi.

Visit our website at
www.penguinputnam.com

ISBN: 0-515-13417-1

A JOVE BOOK®
Jove Books are published by The Berkley Publishing Group,
a division of Penguin Putnam Inc.,
375 Hudson Street, New York, New York 10014.
JOVE and the "J" design
are trademarks belonging to Penguin Putnam Inc.

PRINTED IN THE UNITED STATES OF AMERICA

10 9 8 7 6 5 4 3 2 1

PROLOGUE

This was the first day they walked down Front Street together as husband and wife, acknowledged by people they passed as such, each going to their own office for their day's work. They came to the office of the *Kingdom Nugget* first and stopped there.

Lance had tried briefly to talk Dulcy into giving up the paper after they were married, but learned very quickly that his then wife-to-be had a mind of her own.

"I came here to run the paper and make a go of it, Sam," she said. "I can't give that up just because we're getting married. I hope you'll understand and not ask me to do that, just as I would never ask you to give up your badge."

He'd kissed her then, and he kissed her now, causing her to blush prettily.

"Mr. Lance," she said, pushing him away, "we're out in public."

"And you're my wife," he said, "and I'm the Marshal.

1

The Marshal can kiss his own wife in public."

"Is that a new law?"

"Well," he said, "if it ain't, it damn well should be." He pulled her to him and settled for a hug before she went into her office and closed the door behind her. He stood just for a moment to watch her through the glass, then turned and continued on to his own office. He couldn't believe his luck that this beautiful creature, almost fifteen years his junior, had chosen him.

It was a quiet day for Lance and Todd and around dinnertime the Marshal left his deputy at the office to go and see if his new wife wanted to have dinner with him.

He entered the office of the *Kingdom Nugget* and found it oddly quiet. The printing press was usually going at this time of the day, but today it was silent. Harvey, the press operator, was not there but Lance could see into his wife's office where she was seated at her desk. He walked to the office door and knocked. She turned, saw him, smiled widely, and waved him in.

She met him at the door with a hug and a kiss and he held her tightly for a few moments before letting her go.

"Why is it so quiet? Where's Harvey?"

"Slow news day," she said. "We're not ready to print, yet. I let Harvey go and get some dinner."

"And you? Can you leave for dinner?"

"Dinner with my husband? Definitely."

They locked the door and walked to their favorite little café on a side street and away from the mainstream of town.

"Mr. and Mrs. Lance," the middle-aged waitress

greeted them with a smile. "I have your table waiting."

"Our table," Dulcy said, hugging her husband's arm as they followed the waitress.

"There are certain advantages to being married to the Marshal," Lance told her.

"So you've told me over and over again, Marshal," Dulcy said. "But now we're married, so you can stop trying to prove yourself."

"I don't know if I'll ever be secure enough to do that, Mrs. Lance. There's always a chance that you could get a better offer."

She squeezed his arm and said, "Never."

Steve James watched Lance from a doorway across the street. He made his living with his gun, but he considered himself smarter than the average gunman. He knew he shouldn't go up against Sam Lance alone. He thought he could take him, but just on the off chance that he couldn't, he needed somebody to back his play.

He also needed an edge, and while watching Lance kiss his wife, he thought he had probably found it.

He gave Lance enough time to put some distance between him and the newspaper office before he stepped out of the doorway and crossed the street to see what the situation in the office was.

Steve James was nothing if not thorough when he was planning his play.

Later that evening Marshal Lance walked to the newspaper office to walk his wife home. He was surprised at how giddy he was, like a schoolboy, as he anticipated seeing her again. Would they always be this way?

As he approached the newspaper office he looked up and down the street. The office was on Front Street, but on a corner. He was able to see the window and even though it was getting dark there was apparently no light burning inside. That was unusual, and odd. That meant he could not see into the storefront, but that he could be seen from inside as he crossed the street.

There was no pedestrian traffic, which was also odd at this time of the day. If there was one thing Sam Lance had found out over the years it's that people can sense when there's trouble brewing, and if they're smart they stay away.

There was entirely too little happening on the corner out in front of the *Nugget*. Lance took stock of the situation quickly. There were no open windows in the immediate area, but there were several doorways he could not see into, where a man could have been hidden. He didn't see that he had any choice, though. If there was someone in the newspaper office looking out, waiting for him, it meant that they had Dulcy. This was what every lawman dreaded, that someone would use his family against him. Lance and Dulcy had only been married a day, and already it was happening, and he had no choice but to walk into it with his eyes open, and hope for the best.

He had to hope that Dulcy would be smart enough to give him the moment he'd need to save them both.

What Lance was unaware of at this point was that Steve James had placed a man in a doorway across the street from the newspaper office. Once Lance stepped into the street they'd have him in a cross fire.

As far as James and his extra gunman were concerned, the Marshal was a dead man.

Inside the office of the *Kingdom Nugget* Steve James watched from the window as Sam Lance reached the corner, and hesitated.

"What's he waitin' for?" he asked, aloud.

Standing in front of him Dulcy Lance bit her lip and then said, "My husband is not a fool. He knows something's wrong."

"You think so?"

"I know so."

James looked over at Harvey, who he had bound and gagged and stuck in a corner.

"It don't matter," he said to Dulcy. He put his nose into her hair and pressed himself against her from behind. She could feel the bulge in his pants pressing against her buttocks. "He has to cross the street, anyway, if he wants to find out just what's wrong."

"He won't," she said. "He's too smart."

"He's smart, all right," James said, "but he's married, little lady, and that gives him a weakness."

Dulcy cursed herself for not recognizing Steve James for what he was the first time he'd entered the office with some lame questions about printing an ad. When he returned an hour later he wasted no time producing his gun and telling her to tie Harvey up. He told her he would check the knots and they had better be tight. As she tied Harvey, and apologized for how tight she was making his bonds, she knew that this man was going to use her against her husband. She and Sam Lance had not even been married long enough to discuss this possibility, but they both knew it existed. What they didn't know was that it would rear its ugly head so soon.

She only hoped she was up to it.

"There, see?" James said, into her ear. He slid one hand around her so that he was cupping one of her breasts in his hand. "Here he comes, crossing right over. Let's go out and meet him, shall we?"

When the door opened and Steve James came out with Dulcy in front of him Lance noticed two things. One, that James—whose name he didn't know at the time— was holding on to one of his wife's breasts and two, Dulcy looked afraid, but not panicked.

"Right there, Marshal," James said. "Stop right there."

Lance stopped in the middle of the street. Instinct told him that while he was facing one gun he had to have his back to at least one other. He wasn't sure about this, but he was going to play it that way.

"Who are you?" Lance asked.

"That don't matter. What matters is that I got your wife."

"What do you want?"

"Me? I wanna make a name for myself, like everybody else."

"And do I get to know who I'm facing?" Lance asked.

"Sure, Marshal," James said. "A man's got that comin', don't he?"

Lance waited.

"My name's James, Steve James."

"Never heard of you."

"Ain't nobody heard of me," James said, "but they will, after today."

"Oh, that's right," Lance said, "you'll be the man who hid behind a woman to shoot down a lawman—right?"

"I ain't gonna hide behind your wife, Marshal," James said.

There were eyes watching them, Lance knew, but had people stayed off the street anticipating this? They'd learned a lesson from the past, learned to sense when trouble was brewing. But that didn't mean they didn't want to watch.

"What are you doing with her, then?"

James moved his hand from her breast to her chin and cupped it.

"She's real pretty, ain't she?" James asked. "I just wanted to meet her, but now that I have I think that after I kill you I'll take her to my room and have her once or twice. She any good, Marshal? She worth more than one poke?"

"Friend," Sam Lance said, "you ain't gonna live to find out."

Lance tensed. If James really wanted to get a reputation out of this he was going to have to come out from behind Dulcy before he fired his gun. He'd need to be out in the open when he did it, or the stories would all say he hid behind a woman. As long as he did that nobody would remember insignificant little facts like he had help, or that he'd started out holding her in front of him.

He listened intently hoping that he'd hear the sound of a hammer cocking behind him, or a footfall, or some giveaway. He watched Dulcy, who—God bless her—was looking him straight in the eye. He knew that when she did that she was going to willfully have her way.

"Dulcy," he said aloud, "don't."

"Huh?" Steve James said. "Don't what?"

James already had his gun drawn behind Dulcy's back. He knew he could shove her out of the way and gun her husband down in one quick move. Oswald, the man he had paid to back him up, would step into the street and fire at the same time. Stories would be told how James had been smart enough to catch the great Sam Lance in a cross fire, totally out-thinking the lawman.

"Okay, Missy," James said, moving his hand to Dulcy's arm, "it'll be over in a minute."

He gave Dulcy a shove, but she did something he didn't expect. Instead of just falling to the ground as he shoved her she reached out and grabbed hold of his left arm and held on. Thrown off balance, James fought to retain his footing.

In that split second Sam Lance drew and turned around. He saw the second man stepping into the street and raising his gun, but Dulcy's move had caught this man's eye, as well. Before he could recover from that instant of distraction, Lance fired. The bullet punched into the man's chest, just below the hollow of his neck. He gagged, staggered, and felt all of the strength leave his body.

Lance turned back to Steve James, who had caught his balance and was shaking Dulcy's hold off so he could fire. Lance hurriedly squeezed off the shot that changed his life forever. . . .

ONE

As Clint Adams rode into Denver he had the distinct feeling of coming home. The only other town that gave him the same feeling was Labyrinth, Texas. It was in these two towns—Denver significantly the larger of the two—that he had the most friends in one place.

Two friends he was looking forward to seeing in Denver were Talbot Roper, generally considered the best private detective in the country—even Allan Pinkerton could not argue with that—and Bat Masterson. Clint knew that Bat had come to Denver several months ago to open a gambling house called the Sportsman. He was looking forward to seeing it. He hadn't seen Bat much since they had both gone to Fort Worth to see Luke Short's place, The White Elephant Saloon.

Clint directed his Darley Arabian, Eclipse, to the Denver House, the hotel he used whenever he was in town. It had its own livery stable, so he was able to turn Eclipse over to them right out front and walk into the

11

lobby carrying his saddlebags and rifle. On occasion he'd had desk clerks who recognized him, but this time neither he nor the clerk recognized the other. However, it was clear from the way the clerk reacted when he signed the register that he recognized his name.

"Mr. Adams," the man said. "Nice to have you with us again. Your usual room?"

"Yes, please."

The clerk handed him the key to a two-room suite and said, "Enjoy your stay."

"Thank you. Would you tell the dining room I'll be down for dinner in an hour?"

"Of course."

Clint took his saddlebags up to his rooms, where he took a quick bath before coming down for dinner.

After a thick steak in the Denver House dining room— one of the best restaurants in Denver—Clint went outside, had the doorman get him a cab, and asked the driver, "Do you know where The Sportman's Club is?"

"Bat Masterson's place? Yes, sir."

"Good, let's go."

When they stopped in front of The Sportman's Club Clint was suitably impressed. Not as ostentatious as Luke Short's place, it still presented quite a facade. Clint was anxious to see what was going on inside.

He paid the driver and went inside.

"Bat," Carl Evert said, "Mr. Delaney wants another five thousand dollars credit."

Bat looked at the pit boss and asked, "How much is he in to us tonight?"

"Thirty thousand."

"Keep approving him up to fifty, then cut him off until he pays."

"Yes, sir."

Bat returned his attention to his dinner as the pit boss withdrew. He had half his steak left and most of his vegetables. He still hadn't found a cook he was satisfied with. The steak was overdone, the potatoes underdone. He was going to have to let this one go—the third cook in as many weeks. The gambling was the most important part of his operation, but that didn't mean he could afford to serve bad food.

He pushed the plate away, wondering if he should go to Delmonico's, or over to the Denver House.

"I'm looking for Bat Masterson," Clint told the bartender.

"He's the boss."

"I know."

"Everybody's always lookin' for the boss," the barkeep said. "You lookin' to get a line of credit approved?"

"No," Clint said, "I'm just looking for an old friend."

"You and the boss are friends?"

"That's right."

"What's your name?"

"Clint Adams."

The bartender, a young man in his twenties wearing

a white shirt and black vest, opened his mouth and stared.

"You're the Gunsmith!"

"Shh," Clint said, "not so loud."

The barman lowered his voice. "The boss said you'd show up sooner or later. He said you drink on the house."

"In that case I'll have a beer," Clint said, "and then you can point me in the right direction."

"One beer comin' up," the bartender said, "and the boss's table is all the way in the back."

"All the way in the back" was a long way from the looks of it, so Clint was glad he was getting a beer. This bartender was one of two working an extremely long bar that, from the looks of the business they were doing, probably should have had three men working.

"Here ya go," the bartender said, putting a frosty mug in front of Clint.

"Thanks. What's your name?"

"Cole, my name's Cole."

"Glad to meet you, Cole."

"It's a real pleasure, Mr. Adams. You want me to have somebody go and get Bat for you?"

"No, that's okay," Clint said. "I'll finish this beer and then maybe take another one with me to the back. I just want to look the place over first."

"Look all you want," Cole said. "Everybody in the place has a standing order that you get what you want whenever you're in here." Cole leaned over the bar. "That includes all the girls."

"Thanks, Cole," Clint said. "That's good to know.

Looks like you've got some more customers."

"Just let me know when you want that second beer," Cole said, and then moved down the bar to take care of the new customers.

Clint picked up his beer, turned his back to the bar and leaned against it. It looked as if every gaming table in the room—blackjack, faro, roulette, poker, red dog—was full. From the smells in the air Bat also had a restaurant going. If that was as full as the bar and the games, he had a gold mine on his hands.

The girls circulating around the room were all under thirty, some closer to twenty, and all stunning in their own way. Bat seemed to have every like and dislike covered. There were blondes, brunettes, redheads, oriental girls, and black ones. They were tall, short, had long legs or big breasts, short hair and long, high cheekbones, plump cheeks, full lips and thin. Every man's taste seemed to be covered.

He finished the beer and returned the empty mug to the bar. Cole was right there.

"Another one?"

"No, thanks," Clint said. "Maybe later. Right now I'll go and find Bat."

"You want some advice?"

Clint stopped and looked at the young man. "Sure."

Cole leaned on the bar and lowered his voice. "Don't eat the food here."

TWO

"Still not finishing your meals?" Clint asked. "What would your mother say?"

Bat looked up and broke into a smile. He leaped to his feet and pumped his friend's hand.

"It's about time you showed up," he exclaimed. "We've been open three weeks."

"Is that all?"

"Well, we had some problems that delayed the opening, but we're up and running now."

"Except for the food?" Clint asked, indicating Bat's half-eaten steak.

"I don't know what it is," Bat complained. "I can't find a good chef."

"I know," Clint said. "I was warned."

Bat frowned. "By who?"

"I can't say," Clint answered. "You'd fire him."

"No, no, he'd be right. Why would I fire someone for being right?"

"Just the same—"

"Oh, forget it. Sit down, sit down. I can at least get us some drinks."

They sat and Bat waved a hand. Immediately, one of the women Clint had watched working the floor hurried over. She was a brunette, tall, pale, smooth-skinned, with long legs and high breasts.

"Daphne, would you get us a couple of beers, please?"

"Sure, Bat," she said, touching Bat's shoulder before leaving.

"Bat—"

"No, no, nothing's going on," Bat insisted. "In fact, nothing is going on with any of the girls. I'm too damned busy."

"I can imagine," Clint said. "Must be hell trying to run a successful place like this."

"What makes you think it's successful?"

"Well, there's hardly any elbow room at your bar and your gaming tables are full."

"Yeah, now," Bat said, "but they're empty more hours than they're full, and my dining room is always empty."

"Got any partners?"

"No!"

"Well," Clint said, "at least you learned something from some of Luke's exploits."

Their friend Luke Short had exhibited dismal taste in partners in almost every one of his business ventures.

"I don't need a partner," Bat said, then added, "that is, unless you want to buy in."

"No, not me," Clint said. "I'm not in the market for a business, right now."

"What brings you to Denver, then?"

"I came to see you."

"Well, while you're here you'll eat and drink—well, drink on the house. I don't think you'll be wanting to eat here. Unless you'd like to try a steak?"

"Had one already."

"Where?"

"At the Denver House."

"Was it good?"

"Delicious."

Bat looked down at his half-eaten steak with an expression of distaste. Luckily, at that moment Daphne appeared with their beers.

"Thank you, sweetheart," Bat said. "By the way this is my friend Clint Adams. His money is no good here, understand?"

"I understand, Bat." She smiled at Clint. "I'm Daphne."

"Just call me Clint."

"If you gents need anything else just let me know," she said, and flounced away to continue working the floor.

"The girls are all beautiful," Clint commented.

"What the hell good is an ugly saloon girl?" Bat asked. "I learned that lesson a long time ago, too."

They sat and drank their beers, catching up for a while before Clint asked, "So your biggest problem right now is finding somebody who can cook a steak?"

"That's one of my problems, yeah, but you don't want to hear about that. Hey, you want to play some poker?"

"Your tables are pretty full—"

"No, no not at a house table," Bat said. "I can put

together a game for us in no time, in a private room."

"Sounds good," Clint said, "but not tonight. I'm beat."

"You want me to send Daphne to your room when she gets off tonight?"

"As tempting as that is," Clint said, "I think I'm even too tired for that."

"Tell you what I'll do," Bat said. "I'll set up a game for us tomorrow night. You came here to gamble, right?"

"Why else would I come?"

"Exactly," Bat said. "Where are you staying, the Denver House?"

"Yes."

"We should move you to a room right here. I've got a couple I keep for big gamblers."

"Well, give them to big gamblers, Bat," Clint said. "I'll just stay at the Denver House. It'll be quieter."

"That's what you're looking for in your old age, Clint?" Bat asked. "Quiet?"

"It's what I'm looking for tonight, Bat," Clint said, standing up. He put his hand out and his friend shook it. "I'll come by tomorrow."

"We'll have dinner," Bat said, "only not here."

"You pick the place," Clint said. "Leave a message at my hotel and I'll be there."

"You're on," Bat said. "Damn, it's good to see you. Now if Luke and Wyatt would walk through the door, and my brother Jim, the gang would all be here."

"Well, for the time being you might have to settle for me, old friend," Clint said.

"That ain't settlin', old friend," Bat said, slapping Clint on the back. "See you tomorrow."

Clint waved and made his way through the crowd of gamblers.

He was getting ready for bed some time later when there was a knock at his door. Gentle, quiet, but insistent. He grabbed his gun from his holster and walked to the door. He cracked it and looked into the well-lit hall. Standing out there in all her long-legged, high-breasted glory was Daphne, the saloon girl. He guessed that his friend didn't believe that he was quite that tired.

THREE

"Good evening, Daphne," Clint said, holding his gun behind his back as he swung the door open.

"You're Clint Adams," she said.

"I know," he said, "and you're Daphne. We were introduced at The Sportman's Club."

"Not properly," she said. "I mean, I didn't know who you really were, at the time."

"And now you do?"

"Yes," she said, excitedly, "you're Clint Adams . . . the Gunsmith!"

"Oh. Did Bat send you up here?"

"Bat? No, he doesn't know I'm here."

"Are you sure?"

She looked up and down the hall and said, "Can I come in? I'm a saloon girl, but standing out here in the hall makes me feel more like a whore."

"I'm sorry," he said. "Uh, sure, of course you can come in . . . unless you'd rather go downstairs to the bar."

"The bar?" she asked. "In the Denver House?" Her

eyes were so wide she suddenly looked twenty, even though Clint was sure she was closer to thirty.

"You've never been in the bar here at the Denver House?"

"No."

"Well, let's go, then."

She looked down at herself. She was still wearing the sequined dress she wore on the floor of the Sportsman, having thrown a shawl over it.

"But . . . the way I'm dressed."

"You look great."

She must have touched up her makeup before she came to the hotel, because her face looked flawless. She had a very wide mouth, and beautiful white teeth.

"That smile will light up the place. Are you game?"

"I suppose . . ." she said. "As long as they don't throw me out."

"Don't worry," he said. "You'll be with me. Nobody's going to throw you out. I just need to pull on my boots. Come in."

She entered the room, leaving the door ajar. Clint sat on the bed, pulled his boots on, then strapped on his gunbelt.

"Ready?"

"Do you wear your gun all the time?" she asked.

"I wear a gun all the time," he said. "This one, or another one. Does it bother you?"

"No," she said, "I'm around guns all day. They don't bother me. I just can't imagine never being without one. What about when you sleep?"

"There's always one within reach. Shall we go?"

"Yes," she said, "and thank you."

They went down to the lobby, walked across and entered the Denver House bar. It was late, and the only people there were guests, a few men who perked up as soon as Clint entered with Daphne on his arm.

Clint led her to a table and then asked, "What would you like? I'll go to the bar and get it."

"Well," she said, "this is a switch, being waited on. I'll have a brandy."

"Then I'll have one with you."

He excused himself and went to the bar.

"What can I get for you, Mr. Adams?"

Clint didn't recall ever having seen the bartender before, but the Denver House staff was very good at their jobs.

"Two brandles, please."

"Coming up," the man said. He poured two glasses from a decanter and set them in front of Clint. "Is Napoleon all right?"

"Perfect, thanks."

Clint carried the glasses back to the table, put one in front of Daphne and then sat across from her with the other one. She sipped hers and nodded approvingly.

"Napoleon," she said. "It's wonderful."

"You know your brandy," he said. "I wouldn't have known the difference."

"I'm sorry," she said. "I'm not as wide-eyed as I came across upstairs."

"I didn't think you were."

"I just couldn't believe my luck that you had come to town now, of all times."

"Why is now so special?"

She put her glass down and assumed a very serious posture.

"I have a friend in town I would like you to meet."

"And who's that?"

"Do you know the name Sam Lance?"

"Of course I do," Clint said. "Lance was the Marshal of Kingdom for a long time, before the town went bust. Whatever happened to him?"

"He's the friend I want you to meet," she said.

"He's in Denver? Carrying a badge?"

"I'm afraid Sam hasn't carried a badge for a long time, Clint," she said. "Not since the . . . accident."

"The accident?" Clint repeated. "I don't recall hearing about an accident."

"Then perhaps I should tell you about it," she said. "It should help make more sense of my request."

"It happened five years ago," she explained. "It was just after Sam married Dulcy. In fact, it was the day after their wedding."

"What happened?"

"A man named Steve James decided to try Sam on the street, but he decided he needed an edge or two. He put a man in a doorway on the other side of the street to help him with Sam."

"I heard about Sam and Steve James facing each other," Clint said. "But I never heard the whole story."

"Well, I'm telling you the whole story. Steve James

took Sam's wife as a hostage," Daphne said. "She ran the newspaper, and James walked in there and grabbed her. He brought her out onto the street with him and faced Sam from behind her."

"Jesus," Clint said. "What happened? I heard that Sam killed Steve James in that gunfight."

"He did," Daphne said, "but Sam also killed Dulcy, that day—and, I think, himself."

FOUR

"It was a stray bullet," Daphne went on. "Sam heard the man behind him, turned, and killed him. Then he turned to face Steve James. James pushed Dulcy away and drew, but Dulcy hung onto his arm. Sam didn't know that. He drew and fired twice. His first bullet hit Dulcy, killing her instantly. The second bullet killed Steve James. He walked up to James's body, then, and emptied his gun into it. Then he took Dulcy into his arms in the middle of the street and just held her and cried.

"When he finally stood up he was carrying Dulcy, but he left in the street behind him his gun and his badge. He never picked either one up again."

Clint shook his head as Daphne finished her story.

"I heard he gave up being a lawman after that fight," he said, "but I never heard the rest."

"He's never been the same since, Clint," Daphne said.

"And he's in Denver?"

She nodded. "I saw him two weeks ago. I came here

29

three weeks ago to work for Bat. I didn't know Sam was here, too."

"What's he doing here?"

"As far as I can see," she said, "he's drinking."

Clint went to the bar to get Daphne another brandy, and himself a beer. When he returned to the table she took up her story again.

"I saw him on the street one day and followed him," she said. "All he did was go from saloon to saloon, drinking. Finally, he was staggering so bad he fell over."

"Did you help him?"

"Not exactly."

"What do you mean?"

"I thought he would be mortified if I went over to him to help him," she said, "so I paid a man to help him up, find out where he lived and take him home. I followed them to make sure the man did what I paid him to do."

"Where was home?"

"Some flophouse down by the docks, I'm afraid," she said. "Sam looks like he's really in a bad way, Clint."

"And what do you want me to do, Daphne?"

"I want you to help him," she said.

"Why me?"

"Because you know what it's like to have a reputation," she said. "I don't know if you know what it's like to lose it and fall a long way, but you can probably imagine."

"I can do more than imagine," he assured her.

"Will you help him?"

"Have you talked to Bat about this?"

"I can't."

"Why not? He's got a reputation, and he's got a business. He could probably give Lance a job."

"He's my boss," she said. "I couldn't ask him that."

"And I could?"

"Well, you are his friend."

"Let me see if I have this straight. You want me to help Lance, dry him out even, and then get Bat to give him a job?"

"That's it exactly."

"Daphne," Clint said, "I could do that, and then Bat could give him a job, but the rest is going to be up to him. He's got to want to stop drinking, and to tell you the truth, I can see why he might not want to. I mean . . . killing the woman you loved it not something you want to remember."

"It wasn't his fault!" she said, with feeling. A few men sitting nearby turned their heads to have a look, and she lowered her voice. "It wasn't his fault, Clint. It was an accident."

"That doesn't really matter, Daphne," Clint said. "It was his bullet that killed her. That's not something he's likely to forget, or forgive himself for."

"You men . . ." she said, shaking her head. "Why do you have to take responsibility for the whole world?"

"Not the whole world," Clint said, "just the people we care about. And sometimes, other people ask us to take responsibility for the people they care about."

"I understand," she said, pushing her chair back. "This is my responsibility, not yours."

"Now hold on," he said. "Don't leave. I didn't say I wouldn't try to help."

"You mean you will?"

Clint hesitated a moment, then said, "Here's what I'll do. I'll go and see him, talk to him, and see what he wants to do."

"You won't tell him about me, will you?"

"No," Clint said. "I'll just accidentally run into him, and recognize him, and start talking to him."

"When can you do this?"

"Well . . . tomorrow," Clint said. "It's a little late now."

"Yes, well . . . tomorrow's all right, I guess."

"Daphne, I have to ask you something, now."

"Go ahead."

"What was there between you and Sam Lance, back in Kingdom?" Clint asked. "Were you and he . . ."

"No!" she said. "Never. Sam was an honorable man. He was married to Dulcy, and that was that."

"Were you . . . in love with him?"

"No," she said, in a less convincing tone. She leaned forward and looked at him. "Clint, I'm doing this because Dulcy was my best friend. I loved her. She'd want me to help Sam."

He studied her for a moment, then said, "All right. I can accept that."

"Then you'll do it?"

"I'll do what I can," Clint said. "That's all I can promise."

"That's all I can ask," she said, happily. "Thank you so much!"

FIVE

Clint had entertained thoughts of taking Daphne back to his room with him, but by the time they finished their conversation he'd resigned himself to walking her outside and putting her in a cab.

They left the bar and walked through the lobby.

"Where are we going?" she asked.

"I thought you'd want to go home," he said. "It's late."

"That's what you thought?"

"Yes."

They reached the front door and stopped. The doorman came over to them.

"Does the lady need a cab?" he asked.

Clint looked at Daphne and she shook her head slowly.

"No," Clint said. "The lady doesn't need a cab."

They turned and walked back across the lobby together to the stairs, and up to his room.

Inside the room he asked, "There was never anything between you and Lance?"

"Never."

"And you just want to help him because you and his wife were friends?"

"Yes. Is that so hard to believe?"

"No," he said. "Not hard, at all."

He slipped the straps of her dress off her shoulders, then slid the dress down to her feet. She stepped out of it, still in her underwear and high-heeled shoes. He finished undressing her and, when she was naked, took her hands and led her to the bed.

"I'll bet you're tired," he said.

"Not that tired."

He kissed her, then held her naked body close, feeling her heat through his clothes. He kissed her neck, her shoulders, her skin smooth as glass and fragrant.

"I must smell like a cow," she whispered. "I usually take a bath after work."

"You smell wonderful," he said, and continued to kiss her. He worked his way down the slopes of her high, firm breasts until he was teasing her nipples with his tongue, biting them, sucking them until they were turgid. She sighed as he kissed the undersides of her breasts, his hands sliding down her body, over her hips, touching her taut butt, then sliding a hand between her legs to find her wet already.

He kissed her belly, ran his tongue through the tangle of her pubic hair. His finger was wet from her and he removed it and replaced it with his tongue.

"Oh God," she said, and her knees went weak. He let her fall back onto the bed, then spread her legs and buried his face in her. He worked at her avidly with tongue and lips and soon her belly started to tremble and her legs went rigid and then she was writhing beneath him, trying not to scream so as not to bring the rest of the hotel down on them . . .

Later she sat atop him, his rigid penis buried deep inside of her. She rode him slowly, almost languidly, her head thrown back, his hands on her, palming her breasts, brushing the nipples with his thumbs, feeling her insides tugging at him, sucking at him, feeling her body begin to tremble again. She pressed her hands down flat on his chest and leaned on him, grinding herself into him as she began to tremble, to vibrate above him, biting her lips, digging her nails into him and then bouncing on him wildly, her breasts bobbing, her hair whipping around, so involved in the sensations that were coursing through her that he doubted she even knew he was there . . . and then, as she was coming down from the waves of pleasure his was suddenly building. She opened her eyes and smiled down at him. She kept moving on him because she could feel him beginning to swell in her and she wanted to make him as happy as he had made her, so she kept riding him, gripping him with her insides, until she literally sucked an explosion from him that rocked the bed and—for him—rocked the entire room . . .

"Well," he said, a little later still, "you were right."
    "About what?"
    "You weren't that tired."
    She was lying on her side with her back to him. He

was stroking her butt, her hip, and she leaned back to look at him over her shoulder.

"I am now, though," she said. "Too tired to go home."

"You can stay here," he said. He reached for the sheet and brought it up to cover both of them. She snuggled her butt up against him until they were spooning.

"You don't mind?" she asked.

"Not at all."

"I'm not sure," she said, "but I might snore."

"If you do," he said, "I'll let you know."

"You're sweet."

He held her and in a few moments her breathing indicated that she was asleep. He buried his face in her hair, inhaling the smell of it, a combination of everything she had done that day, starting with a bath and ending with odors of her job and the sweet and sour smells of their sex . . .

SIX

They made love the next morning and then went to breakfast in the Denver House dining room—another first for her.

"How did you get the job with Bat?" he asked.

"I heard from another girl that he was hiring," she said. "I went and interviewed with him. I guess he liked what he saw."

"He would have been a fool not to."

"He hired a lot of girls, all different shapes and sizes," she said. "You saw last night. Some of them are so beautiful."

"Like you."

"Oh, more beautiful than me," she said. "I'll bet you didn't even notice me last night until I came to your table."

"And I'll bet you didn't notice me until you found out who I was," he retorted.

"Well," she reminded him, "there were a lot more of you there than us."

"That's true."

37

She laughed and dug into her breakfast with the gusto of a woman twice her size.

This time when they walked across the lobby they did end up getting her a cab.

"Will I see you later?" she asked.

"I have to see Bat, so I guess you will."

"And what about Sam?" she asked. "Will you see him today?"

"I'll check the hotel you say he was in, but he may have checked out of there by now," he said. "I'll also check some of the saloons you followed him to."

"I hope you find him today," she said. "The sooner you find him the sooner we can get him off the streets."

Clint helped her into the cab and gave the driver her address.

"I'll see you later, Daphne."

She blew him a kiss as the cab pulled away, the driver flicking the reins to get his horse moving at a lively trot.

He turned and went back into the hotel. He went to the front desk and picked up a message left there for him by Bat. It told him to be at The Sportman's Club at three in the afternoon. That left him some five hours or so to kill, so he decided he might as well get started looking for Sam Lance right away. Daphne's story had succeeded in making him feel sorry for the man, and if he could do anything to get him off the street and out of the bottle, why not? Somebody had done that very thing for him once.

SEVEN

Clint found the hotel where Sam Lance had been holed up but, as he had suspected, the man was gone. He checked with the desk clerk, who verified the fact that a man fitting Lance's description had run out of money and had to leave the hotel.

"Do you know which way he went?" Clint asked.

"Mister," the clerk said, "once they pay up and leave I don't keep track of 'em."

"Okay, thanks, anyway."

As Clint turned to leave, the clerk, a wispy little man in his sixties, said, "Hey, fella?"

"Yeah?"

"He a friend of yours?"

"Used to be, at one time."

"Yeah," the clerk said, "I know what ya mean, long time ago, right? Before he fell inta the bottle?"

"That's right."

"I seen it before," the clerk said, wisely. "Check up the street at the Wayfarer Saloon. I seen him there once or twice bummin' drinks."

39

"Okay, thanks."

"Turn left out the door and go about a block and a half. Can't miss it."

"Obliged."

Clint left the rundown waterfront hotel, made the left and walked to the Wayfarer Saloon. He stepped inside and looked around. He'd never met Sam Lance, but Daphne had described him well enough for him to know the man wasn't there. There were three customers in the place, two sitting at separate tables and one leaning on the bar. Behind the bar was a bored-looking bartender, a big man with hairy forearms and a bushy black beard. Like many bartenders in places like this he looked as if he'd be able to double as a bouncer.

Clint walked to the bar and the barkeep moved nothing but his eyes. He studied Clint for a long moment before asking, "Help ya?"

"Beer."

The bartender seemed satisfied that Clint had money, so he drew the beer and set it before him.

"Pay before ya drink."

Okay, so he wasn't that satisfied. Clint gave him the price of the beer and took a sip. It was steep for lukewarm beer, but then he was really there for information, anyway.

"I'm looking for someone," he said to the man. He chose to stand at the far end of the bar from the other man, which really didn't put him beyond the man's unwashed odor.

"Generally speakin'," the bartender said, "most people who are down here are lost in one way or another."

Again, like most bartenders, this one was a philosopher.

"Well, I'm looking for a specific man. About six feet, sandy hair going gray, early fifties, big man gone to seed a bit."

"Could be lots of men."

"Clerk at the hotel down the street says he saw him in here once or twice."

"Maybe he did," the bartender said. "Seems to me a feller lookin' like that was in here beggin' a drink once or twice."

"You give him any?"

"Once, maybe," the man said. "Made him sweep up for it."

"When might that have been?"

The man shrugged. "Few days, maybe."

"Haven't seen him since?"

"Nope. What's your interest?"

"He's an old friend."

"You gonna try and help him crawl out of the bottle?"

"I was thinking about it."

"Seems to me he was pretty deep into it."

"Well," Clint said, something of a philosopher himself sometimes, "seems to me we're all deep into something at one time or another."

"Ya got that right, mister."

Clint pushed away from the bar and said, "Thanks for the beer."

"You ain't gonna finish that?" the unwashed man standing at the bar asked, hopefully. He was in his sixties, slightly built, almost a twin of the clerk at the hotel.

"No," Clint said, "help yourself."

"Much obliged, mister."

Clint walked the rest of the waterfront without seeing Sam Lance anywhere. After a few hours of looking he decided to head back to his hotel before going over to the Sportsman to meet Bat. He was walking past an alley when he heard someone call out, "Hey, mister."

He turned and saw the unwashed man who had finished his beer at the Wayfarer Saloon.

"I think I can help ya," the man said.

Clint wondered if the man was just going to try to get another free beer out of him. He hesitated, then steeled himself and walked over to the man. His odor was almost overpowering up close.

"How can you help me?"

"The fella you're lookin' for," the little man said. "I can take ya to him."

"How do you know where he is?" Clint asked.

"Him and me, we're friends."

"Friends, huh?"

"That's right."

Clint wondered if Sam Lance had fallen so far that this smelly little man was actually a friend of his.

"When can you take me to him?"

"Right now, if ya want."

"And what's it going to cost me?"

The man's eyes began to dart around, as if he was afraid someone was going to be close enough to hear them.

"W-what's it worth to ya?"

"I get to name the price?"

The little man smiled, revealing ugly, yellow teeth.

"Whatever ya offer me is gonna be more than I got now, don't ya think?"

He had a point there.

"Okay," Clint said, "ten dollars."

"Ten?" the man's eyes widened, as if that were much more than he'd expected.

"Is that okay?"

"That's fine, mister, but, uh . . . when do I get paid?"

Clint took five dollars out of his pocket and handed it to the man.

"Half now, half when I see . . . what's his name?"

"Yer testin' me," the man said, tucking away the five dollars, "but that's okay. His name's Lance, Sam Lance."

"Okay, then," Clint said. "Lead the way."

EIGHT

Back at the Wayfarer Saloon, after Clint had gone, the other two men in the place watched as the smelly man finished Clint Adams's beer. Of course, at that point the two men didn't know he was Clint Adams. To them he was just another mark.

Jack Bludis and Mike Bracken sat at separate tables, but anyone who knew them knew they were partners. But it was for the people who didn't know them that they kept up the pretense of sitting apart.

Once Clint left the saloon both men stood up and walked over to the smelly man, whose name was Billy Drew.

"Hey, there, Billy," Bludis said, slapping the little man on the back. "Who was your new friend?"

Drew looked up at Bludis and flinched. Bludis was a big man who enjoyed picking on little men, and up and down the Denver waterfront there wasn't a littler man than Billy Drew.

"He ain't no friend of mine, Jack," Drew said. "H-he just left a perfectly good beer settin' on the bar."

"Well," Bracken said, "maybe we can help you make friends with him, Billy. Wouldja like that? To have a new friend?"

Bracken was of a type with his friend Bludis, both big men in their thirties who thought that hard work meant takin' other men's hard-earned money away from them.

" 'Specially a new friend who looks like he might have some money on him," Bludis added.

"Hmph," the bartender said. "Didn't bother payin' no money for information."

"You want to make some money, Tor?" Bludis asked. "You might consider closin' up and come with us."

"I close up I lose money," Tor said.

Bludis looked around at the empty saloon and said, "Couldn't tell by me."

"It'll get busy later," Tor said.

"We don't need Tor," Bracken said, slapping Drew on the back while the little man was looking at Bludis. Drew's head swung back to look at Bracken and Bludis laid a hand on his shoulder.

"Yer right, Mike," Bludis said. "We got ol' Billy, here, and he's gonna help us. Ain'tcha, Billy?"

"S-sure, Jack, sure," Billy Drew said, nervously. He licked his lips. "Uh . . . help ya with what?"

"Tor," Bludis said, "give my friend Billy a fresh beer, and bring it over to my table. Come on, Billy. Let's talk."

A little while later Billy said, "I c-can't do that, Jack."

"And why not?" Bludis asked. "I thought you were willing to help us, Billy?"

"Yeah but . . . you know me. I'm a coward. I'll—I won't be able ta do it."

"Sure ya will, Billy," Bracken said. "You know why?"

"W-why?"

"Because we're gonna pay ya ta do it," Bludis said.

"P-pay me?"

"Sure," Bludis said. "You don't think we'd expect you ta help us for nothin', do ya?"

"Well—"

"That wouldn't be fair, would it?" Bludis asked Bracken.

They were sitting with the little man between them, and neither man was very mindful of his odor—but then, neither of them smelled exactly like a bunch of roses, either. The one thing the three men had in common is that they were all dock rats. Bludis and Bracken just happened to be bigger ones.

"Yeah, we're gonna pay ya," Bracken said.

"But if ya still don't wanna help us, Billy," Bludis said, clamping his hand down on the little man's shoulder and squeezing until Drew whimpered, "we're gonna have ta hurt ya."

NINE

Clint knew he was on the docks, and he knew the mentality of the men who lived and hung around there. He'd been on the Barbary Coast enough times to know. However, this little smelly man seemed too frightened to be any danger to him.

He followed the man down the alley and out the back, which put them on a different street.

"What's your name?" Clint asked, as they walked along.

"Billy," the small man said, "Billy Drew." Then, just as an afterthought, he asked, "What's yours?"

"Clint Adams."

The name struck an immediate chord in Billy Drew's mind and he stopped short.

"Something wrong?" Clint asked.

"No, no," Billy said, "I, uh, just didn't think you was somebody so famous."

"You think I'm famous?"

"I know yer reputation, Mister Adams," Billy said. "Yeah, I think yer famous."

"How much farther do we have to go?" Clint asked him.

"Not far," Billy said, "not far, at all."

"You think he's gonna come through fer us?" Bracken asked Jack Bludis.

"Hell, yeah," Bludis said. "Billy's too damned scared not to."

They both looked across the alley, where they had two more men waiting for Billy to lead the stranger there.

"Hope this feller's got enough money on him for all of us," Bracken said.

"He don't have ta," Bludis said. "He just has to have enough on him for us, and we'll throw Lee and Henry a few bucks."

"And Billy?"

"Billy?" Bludis said, looking at his partner as if he'd suddenly sprouted another head. "Billy don't get shit. Oh yeah, wait. Billy gets a whuppin'."

"I like that part," Bracken said. "I like givin' out whuppin's."

"Well then be my guest," Bludis said. "You can give Billy his payoff."

Satisfied that he was not only going to get some money, but that he was going to also get to hurt somebody smaller than him, Bracken settled down with a satisfied sigh to wait for Billy and the stranger.

Billy was suddenly elated, knowing that he was leading the Gunsmith to a meeting with Bludis and Bracken. With any luck Adams would kill both men and they'd never bother him again. And maybe he'd even get that second five dollars from Clint Adams. If he didn't get killed, first.

The whole idea scared Billy, but what scared him even more was having to face Bludis and Bracken again afterward. He knew they weren't going to pay him, and he knew they were intending to hurt him. He also knew there was no way he could get away from them—except to have Clint Adams kill them.

For a moment he thought of telling Adams that he was being led into a trap, but he decided against it. If he did Adams might choose not to go along. No, this way was better. He could tell Adams later that he didn't know where those men came from, or what they had done with poor Sam Lance.

In point of fact Billy Drew knew Sam Lance, but at the moment he didn't know where he was. Lance was a decent guy who once or twice had shared a bottle with Billy. In fact, Billy Drew probably considered good ol' Sam his only friend. 'Course, after Bracken and Bludis were dead if Adams still wanted to find Sam, well Billy would help him. After all, five dollars is five dollars.

"How much farther?" Clint asked.

"Jest around the corner," Billy said. "There's an alley he likes ta curl up in if'n he's got a bottle."

"Does he have a bottle today?"

"Damned if I know," Billy said. "I ain't seen him today."

They turned a corner and Billy pointed to an alley on the right side of the street.

"He could be in there."

"Could be?" Clint asked.

"Well, like I tol' ya, Mister Adams," Billy said. "I ain't seen him all day. But that's a place he likes ta be, for sure."

"I see."

"Can I have my other five dollars now?"

"I think I'll wait to see if he's really in there, Billy," Clint said. "If he's not, then I'd be paying you another five dollars for nothing, wouldn't I?"

"I guess . . ."

"So let's go."

"Huh? Me?"

"Sure," Clint said. "You're coming down the alley with me—unless you've got some reason not to?"

Billy had two good reasons not to, named Bludis and Bracken.

"Billy?"

The little man's eyes were darting around in his head so fast Clint could almost hear them.

"We got something to talk about, Billy?"

"Uh . . . yeah . . ." Billy said, hesitantly, "yeah, Mister Adams, I think we do . . ."

TEN

"Where the hell is he?" Bracken demanded.

"He'll be here," Bludis said.

"What makes you so sure?"

"He's too afraid not to come."

"What if he decided to side with the stranger? Tell him that we're waitin' for him?"

"Then they're both dead," Bludis said. "Just relax, Mike. We've done this before."

"I know," Bracken said, "and I get impatient every time."

"Just think about what yer gonna do with the money."

"Gonna get me a steak, a bottle, and a woman, in that order," Bracken said, happily.

"A woman, or a whore?" Bludis asked.

"What's the difference?" Bracken asked.

"Well, dock rats like you and me, we got no chance with a woman," Bludis said. "That's where there's whores."

"Well," Bracken said, "a whore's good enough fer me!"

•   •   •

Billy Drew thought this really wasn't fair. He'd warned
Adams about Bludis and Bracken and the man was still
making him walk down the alley with him. Where was
the justice in that? How was he going to spend his ten
dollars if he was dead?

"This ain't fair," he muttered.

"Quiet," Clint said. "If you do what I say you'll come
out of this alive."

And if he did come out of it alive? And Adams
didn't? He'd be dead, anyway.

Life just ain't fair.

As they moved down the alley Clint kept his eyes and
ears open. Billy had told him that two men would be
waiting for him, but what if there were more? Billy had
also told him that this actually was an alley that Sam
Lance liked to use. The little man had told both Jack
Bludis and Michael Bracken that, which is why they
picked the place for their ambush. Clint was walking
into the ambush because he believed that Billy Drew
really did know Sam Lance. If he didn't walk down this
alley the two men would probably end up killing Billy,
and Clint needed the smelly little man alive.

He just hoped he wasn't walking into an alley filled
with four, or maybe six men. Since Bludis and Bracken
didn't know who he was, maybe they had decided they
could handle things themselves.

After all, he was only one man.

•   •   •

"Quiet!" Bludis said, in a harsh whisper. "They're comin'."

It was light in the alley so he was able to wave to the two men on the other side of the alley and warn them, as well.

Bracken drew his gun and cocked the hammer. Bludis did the same. Across the alley, Lee and Henry did the same thing.

Clint Adams, keeping as alert as he could, picked up at least two of the distinctive clicks, and knew that guns had been drawn in the alley, and cocked.

"Billy," he said, drawing his own gun, "get behind me."

"Yes, sir!"

With the little man behind him Clint stopped dead in his tracks.

"What's happening?" Bracken asked. "Where are they?"

"Shut up!" Bludis said. "They stopped."

"Why?"

"I don't know why," Bludis said.

"Well, let's go and get them."

"Hold on," Bludis said. "Let Lee and Henry go and get them."

"Good idea!"

Bludis looked across the alley and waved to the other two men to move in.

Davey Lee and Walt Henry left the cover of their doorway and moved out into the center of the alley. They could see the stranger standing there, not moving.

"Best put your gun up, friend," Lee said.

"Why?" Clint asked. "Will you kill me faster if I do?"

"Either way you're gonna die," Walt Henry said, standing shoulder to shoulder with Lee.

"Which one is which?" Clint asked Billy.

The little man peered out from behind Clint and said, "That ain't Bludis and Bracken. They musta got help."

Great, Clint thought. Now he was facing two men with two more probably in hiding.

"You boys don't know what you've gotten yourself into," Clint said. "My business is with two men named Bludis and Bracken. Why don't they come out in the open? Why are you two willing to die for them? Are they offering you enough money to die?"

Both Lee and Henry wondered why this man was so confident while facing two of them.

"We don't know who you are, friend," Lee said, "but right now you're business is with us."

"Big mistake," Clint said. "Big, big mistake."

Bludis, hearing the stranger say their names, swore to Bracken and said, "That little bastard gave us to him!"

"I'll kill him!" Bracken said, starting to stand.

"Wait, wait," Bludis said, putting his hand on his partner's arm, "let's see how this plays out."

"Who are you, friend?" Henry asked. "Don't you know you're facing two guns?"

"My name is Clint Adams, friend," Clint said, "and I've faced two guns and more many times."

"What?" Henry said.

"Adams?" Lee repeated.

"That's right."

"That's right," Billy Drew said from behind him. "He's the Gunsmith, boys. Whataya think now?"

Lee and Henry exchanged a glance.

"If I was you boys I'd take my leave of this situation real quick," Clint said.

The two men were frozen where they were, trying to make up their minds.

"Clint Adams?" Bracken said to Bludis. "The Gunsmith?"

"Shut up," Bludis said. "All that means is that he's probably got more money than we thought he would."

"What are we gonna do?" Bracken said. "Those two can't take him!"

"Let's wait for a move to be made," Bludis said, "and then we'll take a hand. He can't take the four of us."

"I hope you're right," Bracken said.

From behind a group of barrels a man who had been asleep until now awoke to all the shouting. He listened for a moment and, although his head was fuzzy, immediately grasped what was going on. None of the other six men in the alley knew he was there, and that suited him just fine. Now he just needed to find a way out before they did notice him.

"You boys better make up your minds," Clint said. "Leave, or make a move."

The two men realized that in order to leave they

would have to go by Clint Adams. Both of them, knowing the reputation of the Gunsmith as a gunman and a
killer, could not imagine that he would let them go so
easily.

"You'd kill us if we tried to leave," Lee said. "We
got no choice here, Adams."

"I'm giving you a choice," Clint said. "Live or die.
Doesn't sound like a hard decision to me."

Lee and Henry exchanged a glance. They both knew
that if they left and Bludis and Bracken somehow managed to kill Adams, they'd be next. No way they'd pay
them what they promised, and they'd definitely kill
them, instead.

"No choice," Lee said to his partner.

"I know."

"They got no choice," Bracken said.

"I know," Bludis said.

Clint could see that the two men were going to make a
move. They felt they had no other choice.

"Billy," he said, "get on the ground . . . now!"

ELEVEN

All guns were already drawn, so all that remained was to bring them to bear. Lee and Henry began to lift their arms, but they had no chance at all. Clint brought his gun up and shot both of them through the chest. They staggered back, bounced off each other, and crumpled to the ground.

"Now!" Bludis said, and he and Bracken sprang to their feet, hoping to catch Clint Adams off guard.

As Bracken stood, moving to follow Bludis out into the center of the alley, a hand suddenly clamped down on his shoulder from behind and spun him around. A big man stood behind him, sandy hair going gray, disheveled-looking and red-eyed. The specter reached out and grabbed his gun hand with one hand and clipped him on the chin with the other. Bracken's head flew back from the force of the blow and there was a loud sound as his neck snapped. His eyes glazed over and he crumpled to the ground, dead. The disheveled man bent and retrieved the fallen man's gun and then stepped out into the center of the alley.

Bludis moved out into the alley and brought his gun up. Clint saw him immediately and started to bring his gun to bear, but at that moment Billy decided to move. It wasn't much, but it was enough for Clint to step on him and lose his balance. Bludis knew that this was the break he needed, and started to squeeze the trigger.

Clint felt his ankle twist as he stepped on Billy. He fought for his balance, but knew that by the time he regained his balance he'd be dead. He tried to bring his gun to bear, but knew he'd be too late. There had been one man too many in the alley.

He heard the shot, and waited for the impact.

Bludis was shocked, because he heard a shot and hadn't pulled the trigger yet. He could see that Adams still didn't have his balance, and hadn't pulled the trigger. As a chunk of lead hit him in the small of the back, paralyzing him completely, his gun dropped from nerveless fingers and he fell to his knees.

"Wha—?" he said, but was dead before he could get the *t* out.

Clint regained his balance in time to see Bludis fall. He saw the man behind him with a gun in his hand and barely had time to stop himself from shooting.

"That ain't Bracken!" Billy shouted. "That's Sam!"

"I know," Clint said, and put up his gun.

TWELVE

"Let's get out of here!" Billy Drew shouted.

He started to get to his feet. Clint grabbed him immediately and kept him from running out of the alley.

"We're not leaving," he said. "We've got some dead men, here. We need some law."

"I ain't gonna talk to no law!" Billy said.

"Yeah," Clint said, "you are." He released his hold on the little man. "If you try to leave this alley, I'll shoot you."

"That ain't fair!"

"Just stay."

Billy continued to complain, but he stayed. Clint walked over to the fallen men, checked to make sure they were all dead, then looked at the man he assumed to be Sam Lance. Lance was still holding the gun, but he had the look of a man who was about to pass out.

"Take it," Lance said.

"What?"

The man coughed, clearing his throat of phlegm, and said again, "Take it!"

Clint knew he meant the gun and relieved him of it. Once he didn't have the gun anymore Lance slumped, almost fell. Clint reached for him but the other man jumped back out of his reach.

"Sam Lance?" Clint asked.

"Don't touch me!"

"I'm not . . . where's the other man?"

"Over there."

Lance staggered sideways, steadied himself on a nearby wall. Clint moved past him to check on the fourth fallen man. He found that he was dead, but there were no bullet holes in him. From the look of his head, though, he had a broken neck.

Clint turned back to Lance.

"You willing to wait for the law?"

Lance passed a hand over his face and said, "I need a drink. I can't talk to anyone before I have a drink."

"Will you wait for the police if I get you a drink?"

"Yes."

"Billy, come here."

Billy slipped past the dead bodies, walked over to Clint with slumped shoulders.

"Sorry about this, Sam."

Lance looked at the little man and, recognizing him suddenly, said, "Billy? What the hell?"

"We can explain everything later," Clint said. "Billy, listen very carefully to me. Go to the saloon and get a bottle of whiskey."

"I need money—"

"You have five dollars," Clint said. "Get a bottle of

whiskey, get a policeman, and bring both of them back here. Do you understand me?"

"Yeah."

"Don't drink any of the whiskey."

"That ain't fair!"

"Life ain't fair," Clint said. "You come back here with the bottle and a policeman and I'll give you the bottle after I'm through with it."

Billy licked his lips, thinking about the bottle.

"Do you understand?"

"Yeah, yeah, I understand."

"You almost got me killed here by moving at the wrong time," Clint said.

"Hey, I didn't mean—"

"If you come back with the bottle and the policeman, I'll forget all about it."

"I didn't mean it."

"I know," Clint said. "Now, go and do what I ask, and if you're not back here within the hour, I'll come looking for you."

"Mister Adams—"

"Go!"

"I'm goin'!"

He watched the little man run out of the alley, virtually leaping over the dead bodies.

"Once he has that bottle he's gone," Lance said.

"He'll be back," Clint said. "Come on, let's get you a place to sit down."

They moved over to the group of barrels Lance had been sleeping behind and the big man sat down on one.

"Where did you come from?" Clint asked.

"I was sleeping behind these barrels. The yelling woke me up."

"You saved my life," Clint said. "Thanks."

"I killed two men," Lance said. "I haven't killed anyone since . . ." He let it trail off and began to tremble. "I need a drink."

"It's coming," Clint said.

"What the hell were you all doing in this alley?" Lance demanded, as if they had invaded his home.

"Well, I was looking for you," Clint said. "These other men were obviously waiting to rob me."

"Looking for me?" Lance asked. "Do I know you?" He apparently had not heard Clint's name mentioned.

"My name is Clint Adams, Marshal Lance."

"Don't call me that!" Lance shouted, spittle leaping from his mouth.

"Easy, take it easy!" Clint said. "I'm sorry."

"I haven't worn a badge since . . . in a long time."

"I understand."

Lance shook his head, as if trying to dispel a fog from his brain.

"Who are you? Why were you looking for me?"

"My name is Clint Adams," Clint said again, "and I was asked to find you."

"By who?"

"Daphne . . ." It was then Clint realized he didn't know Daphne's last name.

"Daphne?" Lance repeated. "Daphne who?"

"A Daphne you once knew in Kingdom."

"Daphne . . ." Lance said, as if trying to recognize the

name. Then his eyes widened. "Wait, do you mean Daphne Gibbs?"

"I don't know her last name," Clint said. "She a beautiful, tall brunette who says she was best friends with . . . uh . . ."

He stopped, not wanting to provoke a violent response in Lance by mentioning his late wife's name.

"Dulcy," Lance said, bringing the name out himself. "She was Dulcy's best friend."

"Yes."

"Oh God," Lance said, "Daphne's here in Denver?"

"She is."

"And she knows about . . . me? What I've become?"

"I'm afraid so."

Lance closed his eyes and when he didn't open them again Clint realized the man had passed out.

THIRTEEN

Clint was just beginning to worry that Lance was right about Billy when the little man reappeared with a uniformed policeman in tow. It wasn't long after that before the alley was filled with uniforms, and with men removing bodies and, finally, a man in a suit who introduced himself as Lieutenant Stoker.

"You're the man we've been waiting for, I assume," Clint said. He was already late in meeting Bat Masterson at The Sportsman's Club, so it really didn't matter at this point who they had been waiting for.

"That's right," the Lieutenant said. "I'm the one who gets to ask all the good questions."

The Lieutenant was in his forties, and had a very relaxed aura about him. Bodies did not surprise or shock him, he had seen enough of them before.

"So," he said, looking at Clint, Lance, and Billy, "why don't you tell me what happened here? Let's start with your names—except for Billy, here, who I know."

"My name's Clint Adams," Clint said, "and this is Sam Lance."

"Adams? And Lance?"

"That's right."

Sam Lance was remaining silent. Clint had given him just enough whiskey to quiet his shakes, but it was going to wear off very soon. He'd even given Billy a taste.

"You said I could have the bottle!" Billy had complained.

"And you can," Clint said, "when I'm done with it."

The bottle was right now on the ground behind the barrels on which they were sitting.

"Adams," Stoker said, "I know you. The Gunsmith, right?"

"Right."

"And Lance," the policeman said. "I know that name."

"I'm nobody," Lance said, speaking for the first time.

"Maybe now," Stoker said, "but you used to be somebody. I'll remember. Okay, what happened here?"

Clint told the story with no help from Lance or Billy, but did point out that both men had helped him to stay alive.

"So it was an attempted robbery?" Stoker asked.

"That's right," Clint said.

"And you and your two friends here killed them?"

"Billy didn't kill anyone," Clint said. "Lance helped me out and saved my life."

"Can I ask why you were looking for Mr. Lance, Adams?" Stoker asked.

"A friend asked me to look him up."

"For what reason?"

"To try and help him."

Stoker looked at Lance, who was listing to one side, in danger of falling over.

"Your friend looks like he could use some help," Stoker said, "and some food."

"I'm going to buy him something to eat when we're done here," Clint said.

"Least you could do," the lieutenant said. "All right, you can all go. Where are you staying, Mr. Adams?"

"The Denver House."

"And why did you come to Denver originally? To find Mr. Lance?"

"No, I came to see my friend Bat Masterson and his new place."

"The Sportsman," Stoker said. "I've been there. It's no Palace, but it's still quite a place."

"I'll tell him you said so."

"All right," Stoker said, "I guess I know where to find all three of you if I need you. Go on, go."

He stepped aside so the three of them could leave. Clint had to help Lance stand and walked him out of the alley.

"Where's my bottle!" Billy complained.

"It's on the ground behind those barrels," Clint said. "Hang around and wait for the police to finish, and then go and get it."

"What if one of the policemen finds it?"

"I'll buy you another one, Billy," Clint said. "I promise."

"Well . . . okay. You gonna get Sam somethin' to eat now?"

Clint didn't know how to answer. He certainly didn't

want to try to get something to eat with the smelly little man along.

"Yeah, I'm going to feed him."

"Good, he needs it," Billy said. "Sam, I'm sorry—"

"We'll talk later, Billy," Lance said.

"Okay," Billy said, "okay."

"Come on," Clint said to Lance. "Let's get a steak."

"I need another drink."

"I'll get you one with your meal," Clint said. "You need to eat, Sam, and sober up if you're going to see Daphne."

"Who said I wanted to see Daphne?" Lance demanded.

"That's something you can decide later."

"Who asked you for help?" Lance demanded.

"Daphne did, and I agreed to give it to her. That means helping you sober up."

"I don't want to sober up."

"Do you want a steak dinner?"

Grudgingly, Lance admitted, "Yeah, I do."

"Then point the way to where we can get one," Clint said.

FOURTEEN

Lance took Clint to a small café right down on the waterfront, which suited Clint fine. He did not think he would have been able to get the man into a respectable restaurant.

They entered the café and a fiftyish waitress with wide hips showed them to a table.

"What can I get ya, Sam?" she asked.

"You know him?" Clint asked.

" 'Course I do," she said. "Sam used to come in here a lot, but he ain't been in for a while. No money, I guess. You buyin' him dinner?"

"I am," Clint said. "Bring us two of the biggest steak dinners you've got."

"Comin' up," she said. "With all the trimmin's."

"And some whiskey," Lance said.

The waitress raised an eyebrow and looked at Clint.

"You serve beer?"

"Sure do."

"Bring us each a beer with dinner."

"You got it."

Lance sat across from Clint, not looking at anything in particular.

"Lance?"

The man seemed startled and looked at him. The pain in his eyes was almost unbearable.

"I haven't fired a gun in years," he said.

"Well, I'm glad you chose today," Clint said. "I'd have been dead if you hadn't."

"I knew that," Lance said. "I knew I had to pull the trigger. See, there was no other way out of the alley for me. If there had been a door, or a window, you'd be dead right now."

"Then I'm glad there wasn't," Clint said. "About that other man . . ."

"I just hit him," Lance said. "I guess I hit him too hard."

Lance's clothes hung on him like they were too big, but they probably had not always been so. He was a big man, still had wide shoulders and large hands, but he was probably thirty or more pounds from being healthy.

"Look," Clint said, "you saved my life today, so I'm going to give you a choice. If you want I'll buy you this meal and then go and tell Daphne that you don't want to see her, and you don't want any help."

Lance didn't answer.

"Or, after this meal, I'll get you a bath, and some fresh clothes, and I can arrange for you to meet with her."

Lance still didn't answer.

"I can go either way," Clint added.

Finally, Lance looked across the table at him.

"I don't know."

"Well, you don't have to decide right now," Clint said. "Let's eat first, and discuss it later."

For a moment Clint thought the man wasn't going to answer, but then he said, "Okay, sure. I'm obliged for the meal."

"No problem."

"Was that true, what you told the lieutenant?"

"About what?"

"That you're here to see Bat Masterson's place?"

"Yeah, that's true," Clint said. "Bat and I are friends. In fact, I'm supposed to be seeing him right now."

"Sorry to intrude."

"You didn't," Clint said. "Those other fellas did. Did you know them?"

"No," Lance said. "I only know Billy."

"Does he always smell like that?"

Lance stared at him and asked, "Smell like what?"

At that moment the waitress appeared with two huge plates bearing steaks and vegetables.

Lance finished his beer before he finished his food and Clint decided not to buy him another one. He finished his own off when he caught Lance eyeing it.

After they finished their meals he asked Lance if he wanted a piece of pie. He ended up buying him two.

"How was everything?" the waitress asked while Clint paid the bill.

"It was great," Clint said.

"Sam?"

"Very good, Sandra," Lance said.

The woman looked at Clint.

"You gonna clean him up now?"

"I'm going to try, Sandra."

"Bring him back when you do, so I can see what he looks like."

"I will."

" 'Bye, Sam."

"Good-bye, Sandra."

Outside Clint said, "She likes you."

"I hadn't noticed."

"Okay, Sam," Clint said, "what's your decision?"

"About what?"

"Do you want to see Daphne or not?"

Lance thought about it for a while, then said, "I suppose I should. After all, she took the trouble to ask you to come looking for me."

"Okay, then," Clint said. "We'll get you some new clothes, and then I'll take you back to my hotel with me for a bath so you can change."

"The Denver House?" Lance asked. "You're gonna take me to the Denver House looking like this?"

"You'll only be looking like this on the way in," Clint said. "You'll look a lot better on the way out, when we go by the Sportsman tonight."

"Tonight?" Lance asked. "You want me to see her tonight?"

"The sooner the better, don't you think?" Clint asked. "Get it over with?"

"Yeah, you're right," Lance said. "Let's get it over quick."

Clint wondered if Lance was already thinking about diving back into a bottle after he saw Daphne.

FIFTEEN

When Clint walked through the lobby with Sam Lance they attracted everyone's eye.

"Ignore them," he said. "They won't even recognize you when we leave."

As they came near the front desk Clint said to Lance, "Just a second." He went to the desk and told the clerk, "I need a barber sent to my room."

"Yes, sir," the man said. "When?"

"Half an hour."

"I'll have him there." The man looked past Clint at Lance, and then back at Clint.

"Thanks," Clint said, without offering any explanation.

"What was that about?" Lance asked as they started upstairs.

"I've arranged for a barber to come to my room and cut your hair."

Lance touched his hair. "I guess I must look pretty ratty."

"You do," Clint said. "First a bath, then the haircut,

and then the new clothes. After that you'll be a new man."

Lance shook his head and said, "Not as long as I have these old memories."

Freshly bathed and cut and wearing new clothes, Sam Lance did, indeed, look to Clint like a new man. He could not, however, comment on Lance's memories. In fact, the man adamantly refused to ever talk about his wife. The only time he'd mentioned her name was that one time in the alley.

"How do I look?"

"Great," Clint said.

Lance was wearing new Levi's, a new cotton shirt, and a new pair of boots. None of the clothes were expensive.

"How do you feel?"

"Clean," Lance said.

"And sober?"

"I've got the shake, on the inside."

"Sam, are you as bad as Billy is with the whiskey?"

"No," Lance said. "There are some days I don't drink at all . . . and then . . ."

"And then what?"

"And then I start to remember again . . . and I take a drink. Then I'll drink for days, maybe even weeks, and then stop again."

"Do you think you could ever stop for good?"

"If I had a good reason to," Lance admitted, "but I really can't think of one."

"Well," Clint said, "maybe Daphne can give you one. Are you ready to go and see her?"

Lance dried his sweaty palms on the sides of his new pants.

"Maybe we shouldn't bother her where she works."

"It's okay," Clint said. "Her boss is a friend of mine. Come on, let's go."

Clint had bought Lance a new jacket, and helped him put it on.

"You look . . . presentable," Clint said.

"That's a lot better than I've looked for months."

As they walked through the lobby Lance said to Clint, "You were right."

"About what?"

"They don't recognize me on the way out."

"The clothes and the haircut."

"And the fact that I'm clean," Lance pointed out. "I haven't been this clean in a long time."

They went outside and had the doorman get them a cab.

"The Sportsman's Club," Clint told the driver.

"Yes, sir."

In the cab Clint asked Lance, "Have you been to The Sportman's Club?"

"No," Lance said. "I would never have gotten past the front door. I've seen it, though . . . once. I don't really leave the waterfront much."

"How long have you been in Denver, Sam?"

"I'm not sure," Lance said. "A long time, I think. Over a year."

"Where were you before that?"

"Drifting," the old lawman answered. "After Kingdom I just . . . drifted."

"So you left Kingdom before the town . . . well, closed." He'd almost said "died."

"Kingdom closed for me a long time ago."

"You know," Clint said, "the way I hear the story it really wasn't your fault—"

"Stop!" Lance said. He said it loud enough for the driver to hear, and he reined in his horse.

"Change your mind?" he asked.

"Just wait a minute," Lance said. He looked at Clint. "If you're gonna try to talk to me about . . . the past, I'm gonna get out right now. It's your choice."

"Well," Clint said, "I think the choice is yours, Sam, but I'll go along with you."

"Fine," Lance said. To the driver he said, "Drive on."

They rode in silence for a while and then Clint said, "But if you're not willing to discuss the past, I wonder what you and Daphne are going to have to talk about."

SIXTEEN

Bat spotted Clint and Sam Lance as soon as they walked into his place.

"You didn't get my message this afternoon," he said to Clint.

"I got it, but something came up. Bat, meet Sam Lance."

"Lance," Bat said, absently, but then suddenly the name rang a bell and he looked at the man. "*The* Sam Lance, Marshal of Kingdom?"

"A long time ago," Lance said.

"Pleased to meet you," Bat said, extending his hand. After a moment Lance took it.

"Drink?" Bat asked.

"Yes," Lance said, just as Clint said, "No."

"Which is it?" Bat asked.

"It's no," Clint said. "Where's Daphne?"

Bat looked surprised. "Why are you looking for Daphne?"

"Mr. Lance is an old friend of hers."

"Is that a fact? She hasn't come down yet. I suppose she's still getting dressed."

Clint looked around. The Sportsman was packed, every table filled whether it was gaming or just drinking.

"Can we get a table?" he asked.

"Mine. Follow me."

"And some coffee?"

"I'll arrange it."

They followed Bat to his table in the very rear of the place.

"Have a seat, Sam," Clint said. "I'll be right back. No drink, okay?"

"Sure."

Clint put his hand on Bat's shoulder and the two men moved away, out of Lance's hearing.

"What's going on?"

Briefly, Clint explained about agreeing to help Daphne, and what it had all led up to.

"Guess that explains why you didn't show up today," Bat said. "I've got a game set up for us tomorrow."

"Tomorrow's fine," Clint said. "Here?"

"No, the Palace."

"The Palace Theater?"

"That's right."

"Must be a good game."

"It is," Bat said. "High rollers. You going to be able to make it?"

"I should," Clint said. "I think my part in this is done. It's up to Daphne, now."

"And here she comes now."

Clint looked at the stairs leading upstairs and saw

Daphne coming down. She was wearing another sparkly dress in the same style as yesterday's.

"I'll get the coffee," Bat said.

"I'll get Daphne."

He looked back at Lance, to make sure the man hadn't snagged a drink from a passing saloon girl, then walked across the floor to intercept Daphne.

"Clint," she said, smiling. "Do you have good news for me?"

For his answer Clint pointed to Bat's table, where Sam Lance was sitting, looking lost.

"Oh my God," she said. "He looks so much better."

"A haircut, a bath, and some new clothes."

"Does he know about me?"

"Yes."

"Is he . . ."

"Sober? For now. But I don't believe he wants to stay that way."

"Has he talked about her?"

"He refuses," Clint said. "Blows up any time I try to bring up her name."

"Oh."

They stood there together, watching Lance.

"Should we . . . get him something?" she asked.

"Bat's getting coffee." He looked at her. "Don't you want to talk to him?"

"Yes," she said, "but . . . I'm afraid."

"Why?"

She took her eyes away from Lance and looked at Clint.

"Seeing me will remind him . . . of everything."

"Daphne," Clint said, "he's never forgotten everything. He doesn't need you to remind him of it. He drinks to forget."

"It wasn't his fault."

"He won't listen to that."

Bat appeared at Clint's side. Behind him was a saloon girl carrying a tray with coffee and cups.

"Hello, Elise," Daphne said to the blonde.

"Daphne."

"Mr. Masterson."

"Good evening, Daphne. Are you going to talk to your friend?"

"Yes, sir."

"Why don't you and Elise go on over, then."

"Yes, sir."

Both women walked over to Lance's table. Elise set the coffeepot and the cups down on the table. Daphne sat down across from Lance and started pouring before either of them said a word.

"So what's the story?" Bat asked.

"I told you—"

"I mean, what happens now?"

"Well, she'd like him to stay sober," Clint said. "She'd also like to get him a job."

"Here?"

Clint shrugged.

"He helped you out," Bat said. "Can he handle a gun?"

"Don't know," Clint said. "He might have gotten lucky today. His hands were shaking pretty bad after."

"Maybe he can tend bar?"

"Bad idea."

"Right. How about you? Drink?"

"I could use one."

They turned and walked to the bar.

"How have you been, Daphne?" Lance asked.

"I've been fine, Sam," she said. "I've thought about you a lot . . . since that day."

"Yeah," he said, "that day." He picked up his coffee cup and sipped from it. It was still scalding hot but he didn't seem to notice.

"Sam . . . it wasn't your fault."

She tensed, waiting to see if he would blow up, the way Clint said.

"That's what everyone told me, Daphne," he said, calmly. "I even told myself that."

"And?"

He put the cup down.

"It never helped," Lance said. "It still doesn't."

She reached across the table and put her hand over his.

"It's good to see you."

He closed his hand over hers, squeezing.

"It's good to see you, too."

At the bar Bat said, "I'm gonna buy it."

"Buy what?"

"The Palace."

"You just opened this place."

"I know," Bat said. "My plan is to run this place for a while, then sell it at a profit and buy the Palace. Once

I own it, I'll be the premier sportsman in Denver."

"That's what you want to be now? A sportsman?"

"Why not?" Bat asked. "I want to try some new things." He drank some beer. "I might even start writing."

"Writing what?"

"For the newspapers."

"Which one?"

"I don't know," Bat said. "I haven't decided yet."

This was something Clint had admired about Bat Masterson for years. Although Bat was renowned as a gambler, and for his ability with a gun, he was never satisfied. He was always ambitious, always anxious to try new things.

"We still haven't had much time to talk," Bat said. "It's good to see you."

"And you."

"Think we can manage to stay out of trouble?"

"I don't know," Clint said. "Seems like anytime we're in the same place trouble manages to find us."

"Maybe we can hold it off, this time," Bat said, "although you've had your share already."

"By the way, I met someone today who says he's been here."

"Lots of people have been here since we opened," Bat said. "Who are we talking about?"

"A fella named Stoker, a police lieutenant."

"I know Stoker," Bat said. "He gambles."

"Wins or loses?"

"Doesn't much matter to him," Bat said. "It's the gambling that counts."

"Friend or foe?"

"Customer."

"Speak of the devil."

They both watched as Lieutenant Stoker of the Denver Police approached them.

SEVENTEEN

"Gentlemen," Stoker said.

"Bat," Clint said, "you know Lieutenant Stoker."

"I've had the pleasure," Bat said, and the two men shook hands. "Allow me to buy you a drink, Lieutenant?"

"Why not?" Stoker said. "It's not like I'm on duty."

"Beer?"

"Thank you."

Bat signaled the bartender to bring three more beers.

"Here to indulge?" Bat asked.

"I thought I might try my luck."

"What game?" Clint asked.

"Poker."

"Ah," Bat said.

"Not in your league, I'm afraid," Stoker said, "or yours, from what I hear, Mr. Adams."

"Bat's the poker player," Clint said. "I dabble."

"Don't let him fool you," Bat said. "He's as good as anyone."

"How kind," Clint said.

"Well," Stoker said, "I'm only good enough for the house games. I'm much obliged for the beer, Mr. Masterson."

"Call me Bat," Bat said. "Any friend of Clint's can call me by my first name."

"Is that what he said?" Stoker asked. "That we were friends?"

"Well," Bat admitted, "he said you got along. That's almost the same thing."

"We'll get along," Stoker said, "as long as he doesn't kill anyone else while he's in town."

"I'll do my best to avoid it," Clint promised.

"That's good to hear," Stoker said. "Well, wish me luck." He toasted them both with his mug and made for the poker tables.

" 'Any friend of Clint's'?" Clint repeated.

"Hey," Bat said, "in my business it doesn't hurt to have a policeman on my side."

They looked over to the table where Lance and Daphne were sitting and saw that they were talking in earnest, hands clasped in the center of the table.

"Old romance being rekindled over there?" Bat asked.

"She says no. Claims that she was his wife's best friend."

"Oh, yeah!" Bat said, suddenly. "That Kingdom shoot-out with Steve James."

"You heard about that?"

"Sure," Bat said. "Marshal Sam Lance, killed Steve James and another man, but his wife took a bullet and died."

"A bullet from his gun."

"Ooh," Bat said, as if someone had suddenly hit him in the stomach. "No wonder he's drinking."

"Well," Clint said, "not tonight, anyway."

Clint gave Daphne and Lance what he thought was enough time to catch up and then walked over.

"See if you can get her back to work tonight, will you?" Bat had asked. "I can't pay her to sit around."

"I'll do my best."

He walked over now and asked, "Mind if I sit?"

"I have to get to work, anyway," Daphne said. "Can we talk again tomorrow?" she asked Lance.

"Sure."

She stood up, touched Clint's arm and said, "Thank you."

As she went to work Clint sat in her vacated seat and faced Sam Lance. He picked up the coffeepot to see if there was any left and poured himself some.

"How did that go?" he asked.

"It was good to see her," Lance said, "but it was also hard."

"I can imagine—or maybe I can't. Sorry."

"That's okay."

"You got a place to stay tonight?" Clint asked.

"That alley," Lance replied.

"Not good. Bat's got some rooms upstairs he saves for high rollers. I'll get you one."

"That's okay," Lance said. "I'm already beholden to you and Daphne. Might as well not add Bat Masterson to the list."

"Well," Clint said, "you wouldn't be beholden to him if you worked here."

"Doin' what?" Lance asked. "Maybe I'm sober, Clint, but I'm not ready to strap on a gun, again."

"Bartender?"

"No experience," Lance said. "Besides, have you seen his bartenders? I'm about twenty years too old to fit in."

"Well, take the room for tonight and we'll figure something out tomorrow."

"Why?"

"Why what?"

"Why do you still want to help me?" he asked. "You did what Daphne asked you to do. Why not drop it?"

"I'll tell you why," Clint said. "What happened to you could have happened to me at any time in my life—and it still could. That good enough for you?"

Lance stared at Clint, then nodded and said, "It'll do."

EIGHTEEN

When Clint approached Bat about giving Sam Lance a room for the night his friend said, "Sure, why not? I've got no high rollers in the house tonight. You sure you don't want a room?"

"No, I'll stay at the Denver House."

"Can't blame you for that."

"You solve your chef problem, yet?"

"Maybe," Bat said. "I hired somebody new today. We'll see how it goes for a while. You gonna stay and eat?"

"Well—"

"It would really help me out," Bat said. "I value your opinion. Just have a steak and vegetables, on the house."

"Okay, fine," Clint said, "but not yet. It's still a little too early."

"Just let me know," Bat said. "You can have it in the dining room, or in here. Same goes for your new friend. If I'm gonna give him a room I might as well feed him, too."

"He had a big steak for lunch—in fact, we both did.

I'm sure he won't turn down another one, though."

"Where'd you have a steak this afternoon?"

"A little café on the waterfront. It was really good."

"I wonder if their cook would like a job? You know who it was?"

"Actually, I don't. I know the waitress's name is Sandy, but that's all I know."

"Good lookin'?"

"In a mature way, yeah."

"Not saloon girl material, then?"

"No."

"Well, let's see how my new cook does before I start thinking about another one."

"Bat?"

Both Clint and Bat turned toward the sound of the voice.

"Clint, this is one of my pit bosses, Carl Evert. Carl, Clint Adams, a good friend of mine."

"Happy to meet you," Evert said, as they shook hands. "Bat, I've got a small problem that needs your attention."

"I better take care of this," Bat said. He put his hand in his pocket and came out with a key. "Upstairs, first door on the right. Sheets are clean, so are the towels. You can pump water for a bath and then heat some up down the hall."

"I'll take him up."

Bat went off with Carl Evert and Clint walked back over to where Sam Lance was sitting by himself. He looked around and saw Daphne hard at work at her job. She gave him a smile and a small wave.

"Want to take a look at your room?" Clint asked Lance.

"Sure."

Lance stood up and Clint led the way to the stairs. They went up and Clint keyed the first door on the right and let them in. The room was fairly large, well-furnished and comfortable. The bathtub was in another small room, behind a closed door.

"Never had a bathtub in my room before," Lance said.

"Well, you can take another bath, if you like."

"One should be enough," Lance sad. "For a change I haven't spent the day in a cold sweat."

"That's an improvement."

"There's still time, though."

"You and I have free steak dinners waiting for us in the dining room when we're ready."

"I'm taking advantage—"

"Bat just hired a new cook and he wants our opinion. Wouldn't be polite to turn him down."

"Okay, you've convinced me."

Lance went to the bed and sat down.

"How's it feel?"

"Good," Lance said, "but then I slept in an alley last night."

"You'll get a good night's sleep tonight."

"A bath, a haircut, new clothes, two steak dinners, and a good night's sleep," Lance said. "I don't know that I'll ever be able to repay you, Clint."

"Hey, I'm just doing a favor for Daphne. She's the one you'd have to repay."

"I know what she wants from me," Lance said. "I'm not sure that I can promise it."

"To stay sober?"

Lance nodded.

"I guess you'll just have to take it one day at a time, Sam," Clint said. "That's all any of us can do."

Lance passed his hands over his lips, then pulled it away.

"You want to relax up here for a while or come back downstairs?" Clint asked.

"I think I'll stay up here a little while. Why don't I come down in about an hour for that steak?"

"Fine. I'll meet you at Bat's table and then we'll go into the dining room. It'll be . . . quieter."

Lance knew that Clint meant it would be away from the bar.

"You want me to come up and get you? You don't have a watch—"

"Don't worry," Lance said. "I'll be down there. I've got a clock in here." Lance touched his temple.

"Okay, then," Clint said. "See you in an hour."

NINETEEN

Daphne was waiting at the foot of the stairs when Clint came downstairs.

"What's going on?" she asked.

"Bat gave Sam one of the high-roller rooms for the night."

"You asked him?"

Clint nodded. She kissed him on the cheek, tall enough to do it without having to stand on her toes.

"You're wonderful."

"You think so? Wait until you hear this: Bat's also giving both of us free steak dinners."

Now she frowned. "Has he hired a new cook?"

"Started today. Sam and I are among the test cases, I guess."

"Whatever it's like it'll still be good for him," she said. "I can't thank you enough, Clint. I think he's going to be all right, don't you?"

Oh, boy, Clint thought. She was living in a dream world if she thought one good day could overcome five years of abuse.

"Come sit over here with me for a minute, Daphne."

"I have to work—"

"We can make it look like work," he said. "Come on. I want to talk to you."

They walked over to Bat's table, which she commented on.

"It's okay," Clint said. "I have the run of the place, and you're with me right now."

Tentatively she sat in Bat's chair, which Clint held out for her. He then sat across from her.

"Daphne . . . Sam's been drinking and not taking care of himself for five years," Clint said.

"I know that."

"Well, it's going to take more than one good day to undo all of that," he explained. "Right now he's upstairs craving a drink. In fact, he might have gone out the back door by now."

"Do you think—"

"No, actually I don't think he's done that," Clint said, "but I do know he wants a drink."

"Then a saloon isn't exactly the right place for him, is it?" she asked.

"Well, I think Bat would object to your calling the Sportsman a saloon, but you're right. He's going to meet me down here in about an hour and then he and I will go into the dining room and eat."

"Will you give him a drink?"

"I'll give him one beer, because by then he'll have the shakes. He won't be able to eat unless I give him something."

"And then what?"

"And then he'll go upstairs and try to sleep."

"And tomorrow?"

"I don't know," Clint said. "I can't exactly baby-sit him all day and night for the next . . . however long it takes for him to get himself right. And that's supposing that he wants to get himself right."

"I'll help him, then."

"Good," Clint said, "because he's going to need help for a while."

"But if I want to help him, that won't leave me much time for . . . us."

Clint reached out and took her hand.

"Daphne, I don't think one night constitutes an 'us,' do you?"

She blinked at him for a moment, then stammered, "Oh, well, no, of course not. I—well, I never thought that."

"Good, because since you started this you're the one who's going to have to stick with it. If you leave him alone, he'll go back to the bottle."

"He says he doesn't drink all the time."

"He drinks enough," Clint said. "You better go back to work now. I'll talk to Bat about getting you some time off to work on Sam."

"I can't afford—"

"With pay?"

"You can do that?"

"For a while," Clint said. "All I have to do is stay around Denver for a while and keep Bat busy. He and I will be playing poker tomorrow night at the Palace."

"I guess I can . . . uh, keep Sam busy so he doesn't want to drink, but . . . how?"

"Well," Clint said, "you could do with him what you did with me last night. It sure kept me busy."

She stared at him, mouth agape.

"I was kidding," he said. "Hey? Kidding?"

"I . . . I have to go back to work," she said, standing up. "I'll see you . . . tomorrow, I guess."

He watched as she walked away, thinking that he'd offended her with his bad joke. Oh well, Sam Lance was her responsibility. After tonight he would have done more than his part toward the rescue of Sam Lance. Daphne was going to have to do the rest.

Sam Lance reclined on the bed, fully dressed, staring at the ceiling. All he could think about was that bottle of whiskey they had left in the alley. He wondered if Billy had gone back and gotten it after the police left.

He tried to put the whiskey out of his head, but whenever he did that Dulcy came dancing into his head. It was either think about the whiskey, or think about her, and when he thought about her all he could see was her dead body.

He wondered if there was a back door out of The Sportsman's Club.

TWENTY

"Is there a back way out of here?" Clint asked Bat about an hour later.

"Why? You thinkin' Lance ducked out on you?"

"Well, I was starting to, but there he is."

Lance came down the stairs and shambled over to where Clint and Bat were sitting together. Bat had agreed to give Daphne some time off with pay, providing Clint stayed around long enough for Bat to make back some of the money across a poker table.

"Done," Clint had said.

Now Lance approached and eyed both of them.

"Guess you thought I slipped out the back door, huh?"

"The thought had crossed my mind," Clint said.

"Not mine," Bat said. "I've got faith in human nature. That's why I run a gaming club."

"I'll figure that one out tomorrow," Clint said. "Come on, let's go and eat our free meal."

"Bat," Lance said, "I can't thank you enough for the room and the meal."

"Don't worry," Bat said, as he and Clint made their

way toward the dining room, "it's only free until I get Clint to the poker table!"

"Sounds to me like Bat is going to make you pay for all this one way or another," Lance said.

"Not this steak," Clint said. He stopped trying to saw through it and pushed it away half-finished. "Looks like he hasn't found his cook yet."

"Can you compete with him at the poker table?"

"Hmm? Oh, yeah, Bat and I have played many times. Listen, Sam, that steak we had this afternoon at that café . . ."

"Sure was better than this one, wasn't it?" Lance said, but he kept on eating.

"Was Sandy just the waitress there?" Clint asked. "Or did she cook the meal, too?"

"She's the cook, the waitress, and the swamper," Lance said. "She's got no money to hire any help. Once in a while I'd help out and sweep for her, but—"

"Do you think she'd want a job?"

"A job?" Lance looked down at his steak, and then back at Clint. "Here?"

"Yes, cooking here," Clint said.

"I think she'd jump at it," he said. "Do you think Bat would hire her?"

"Maybe," Clint said, "after we take him there for lunch tomorrow."

"That would be great," Lance said. "I know she's struggling there, plus it's kind of dangerous for her down there. That would help her out a lot."

"Why don't we tell her that you suggested it to Bat?" Clint asked.

"Me? Why?"

"Let's just say I helped you, so you'll be helping her."

"But it's you—"

"What does it matter?" Clint asked. "Don't you want to help her?"

"Well, sure . . ."

"Okay then," Clint said. "Bat's going to ask us how we liked this meal. That's when you tell him about Sandy."

"Oh, I see what you're doing," Lance said.

"You do?"

"I owe Bat, so this is my way of paying him back," Lance said. "At the same time I help Sandy, and then she'll owe me—"

"Whoa, whoa," Clint said, "that's too many people owing too many people to suit me. Let's just say that everybody will be getting something they want. That work for you?"

"Oh yeah," Lance said. "It works for me just fine."

"You want to try a piece of pie?" Clint asked.

"No," Lance said, "but I know where we can get a good slice—and we could take Bat with us."

"Sounds like a good idea to me."

Sandy watched curiously as the three men—Sam Lance, Clint Adams, and Bat Masterson—each had a slice of her pie, a different flavor for each of them. They were the only customers she had.

"Jesus," Bat said, "this apple is great. What do you have?"

"Peach," Clint said.

Bat reached over with his fork to get a piece of the peach and taste it.

"Wow. What do you have?"

"Rhubarb," Lance said.

Bat started to reach with his fork, but thought better of it. "I hate rhubarb."

"You should taste her steak," Lance said. He looked over at her. "Sandy, can you bring Bat a steak?"

"Sure, but—"

"Just bring it," Lance said. "No vegetables. Just bring the steak, huh?"

"Right."

She shrugged and went into the kitchen.

"If her steak is as good as her pie, she's hired."

"If she wants the job, that is," Clint said. "She might not want to give up her own place."

Bat looked around and said, "Oh yeah, I can see how she'd want to hold on to a place like this."

By the time Bat had finished his apple pie, plus Clint's peach, Sandy came back with the steak. She set it down in front of Bat, who took a moment to inhale.

"It smells good," he said.

"Wait until you taste it," Lance said.

They all watched while Bat sliced off a hunk and put it into his mouth. He chewed several times and swallowed, then smiled.

"My God," he said, "that's delicious."

"I told you," Lance said.

Bat cut off a bigger piece and put it in his mouth.

"God, it almost melts in your mouth."

"Sam," Sandy said, "what's going on?"

"Ask Bat," Lance said.

"Mr. Masterson?" she said. "It's an honor to have you—a-and Mr. Adams—in my place, but what's he talking about?"

"Miss . . . Sandy, is it?"

"Yes," she said, "Sandy Kenyon."

"Well, Sandy, have you heard of The Sportsman's Club?"

"That's your place, right? A gaming house?"

"Thank you for not calling it a saloon," Bat said. "It's a gaming house and a restaurant, only I haven't been able to find a good cook."

"Wait a minute," she said, "you're not . . . offering me a job, are you?"

"Sandy," he said, cutting off another slice of steak, "I'm not offerin' you a job, I'm beggin' you to take one." He popped another piece of meat into his mouth and closed his eyes.

TWENTY-ONE

Sandy was to start at The Sportsman's Club the next day.

"How long will it take you to close this place down?" Bat had asked while finishing his steak.

"Consider it closed."

"And how long before you can start at my place?"

"Consider me started."

And so she would arrive at Bat's place early the next morning.

Bat, Clint, and Lance left Sandy's together.

"Sure she doesn't need to be walked home?" Bat asked.

"No, she lives upstairs," Lance said.

"She lives here, too?" Bat asked. "Well, we're gonna have to change that. Can't have my new cook—my new damned good cook—living on the waterfront. Too dangerous. I'll give her a room upstairs."

"One of the high-roller rooms?" Clint asked.

"No," Bat said, "I have plenty of rooms upstairs. I made sure of that when I had it built."

"You want to go back in and tell her?" Clint asked.

"No, I'll tell her tomorrow," Bat said. "Sam, I can't thank you enough for this."

"Well," Lance said, with a nervous look at Clint, "it's just my way of paying you back for your kindnesses."

"My kindnesses?" Bat asked. "Like giving you a free bad steak dinner?"

"How about giving me a free room?"

"Hey, believe me," Bat said. "I owe you, now. Sandy is the final piece to the puzzle of my place."

"So now you can compete with the Palace?" Clint asked.

"The Palace? Oh, hell, no. There's no way I can compete with the Palace, no matter what I have. That's why I want to buy the place."

"But that won't happen for a while, right?" Clint asked.

"Not for quite a while," Bat said, "but my plan is long-range, so I can wait."

Clint looked at Lance.

"How does it feel to help a friend?" he asked.

"Actually," Lance said, "it feels kind of good."

"Yeah," Bat said, "helping friends feels real good— just like I'm going to help myself to some of Clint's money at the poker table tomorrow."

"Keep dreaming," Clint said. "I'm going to head back to my hotel now, and leave you boys to make your way back to The Sportsman's Club."

"Hey," Bat said, "I thought you'd come back and have a celebration . . . uh . . ."

"Drink?" Lance asked.

"Sorry."

"Don't be," Lance said. "A celebration sounds good. I could have coffee, or . . . maybe one beer?" He looked at Clint.

"You know," Clint said, "maybe one beer would be good. On second thought maybe I'll come along, after all."

They got back to the Sportsman and took up a position at Bat's table. They had Daphne bring three beers over to the table. As she set one down in front of Sam Lance she looked at Clint, who nodded. She set it down, smiled and took her leave.

"Here's to the final piece to Bat's puzzle," Lance said.

Bat and Clint lifted their mugs along with him, and when they set theirs down they saw that Lance had finished half of his.

"I'm okay," Lance said, setting his mug down. "I'll take my time with the rest of this and then go to bed."

"Maybe," Bat said, "a saloon is not the place for you to be."

"This is not a saloon," Clint said.

"You know what I mean."

"I'll be fine," Lance said. "In fact, I won't even finish this. I'll just go up now." He stood. "Good night. See you both in the morning."

They both watched Lance walk to the stairs and ascend.

"He's steadier," Bat said. "Did you notice that?"

"Yeah," Clint said, "but it was probably the beer. Let's see how things go tomorrow."

"You gonna stay with him tomorrow?"

"No," Clint said, "like I told Daphne, my part's done. The rest is going to be up to her—and to Sam." He looked at Bat. "Tomorrow is for poker at the Palace."

"Well," Bat said, "that won't be until after dark, actually. I'll probably spend the morning getting Sandy set up in the kitchen."

"In that case I'll get back to my hotel now," Clint said. "I could use a good, long night's sleep. I'll meet you here at . . . six?"

"For dinner," Bat said. "Sandy's first night as cook."

Clint stood up. "You don't have to ask me twice. I've tasted her cooking already, remember?"

"I'll walk you to the front."

They walked together to the front door, Bat greeting some of the gamblers along the way.

When they reached the front Bat asked Clint, "Do you think Lance would take a job from me?"

"A job? Doing what?"

"Well, you mentioned it earlier," Bat said. "Maybe . . . I don't know. Maybe I should just discuss it with him."

"Maybe you should," Clint said. "Maybe he can come up with a job idea, himself."

"Or maybe he'll turn me down."

"And maybe we should just get some sleep and start

all over again tomorrow," Clint said. "Right now my mind is too full of maybes and what-ifs. Good night, Bat."

"Good night, Clint."

TWENTY-TWO

Colton James signed his name in the registration book of the hotel, then signed the next three names, as well: Willis James, Danny James, and Ezekial James.

"All named James?" the clerk said, smiling. "Brothers?"

Colton looked at him without smiling. The clerk was a tall, gangly, bored man who was trying to break the boredom by making conversation with the first guests he'd seen in days.

"We need three rooms."

"Three?"

"Yes," he said, "two of us will share. I will have my own room."

"And which of the others gets his own room?"

"Why is that any of your business?"

"Well . . . uh, it ain't."

"Keys?"

"Sure."

The clerk handed over the keys.

111

Colton turned to his three brothers, handed Willy one key and said, "You share with Danny."

"Why does Zeke get his own room?" Danny demanded.

"Because he smells," Colton said.

"Hey!" Zeke said.

"You got body odors, Zeke," Colton said. "Face it."

"Colt! That ain't right!" Zeke said.

"Here's your key," Colton said. "Go to your rooms."

"When do we look for Lance?" Danny asked.

"Tomorrow."

"Why not tonight?" Willy asked.

Colt James looked at his three younger brothers.

"We've waited five years to catch up to him," he said. "Waiting one more night won't kill you boys."

"Colt—" Zeke started.

"Shut up."

"But Colt—" Danny said.

"Shut up."

"Hey, Colt—" Willy said.

"Shut the hell up," Colt said, "all three of you. Just go to your rooms."

The three brothers picked up their warbags and shuffled up the steps of the waterfront fleabag hotel.

Colt turned and loomed at the clerk.

"Anyplace around here to get something to eat?"

"This late? No."

"I saw a café down the street—"

"She closed down."

"For the night?'"

"For good, apparently," the clerk said.

"When?"

"Just tonight, actually."

"No place else?"

"Not near here," the clerk said, "and not this late. In the morning you could walk a few blocks and find a place."

"In the morning," Colt said. "This is Denver, right? Big city?"

"This is the Denver waterfront," the clerk said. "It's like a small town."

"And are you the mayor?"

The clerk laughed. "We ain't got a mayor, and I got a boss."

"Okay," Colt said. "Maybe you can help me. I'm lookin' for a man."

"What man?"

"Tall, sandy hair maybe going gray now. Early fifties. Looks like he was in good shape, once, but has probably lost a lot of weight."

"Sounds like somebody I mighta seen," the clerk said. "Then again, maybe not. What's it worth to you?"

"Well," Colt said, "if you was to help us, then me and my brothers wouldn't take this fleabag apart, and kill you at the same time."

The clerk swallowed. "W-what?"

"You gonna be here in the morning?" Colt asked.

"Uh, yeah, I work all night."

"Good." Colt put his big hand on the man's bony shoulder and exerted just a little pressure. "I'm gonna give you the night to think it over, and in the morning I'll ask the same question. Okay?"

"O-okay, yeah, sure."

Colt picked up his bag and went up the stairs to find his room.

TWENTY-THREE

When Clint awoke the next morning he decided to make full use of the amenities the Denver House had to offer. He took a long bath, then went downstairs and had a shave and a haircut. After that he went to the dining room and had a big breakfast, including two pots of coffee. He was working on the last cup of coffee when Lieutenant Stoker came walking into the dining room. He looked around, spotted Clint and came walking over.

"Mind if I join you?" he asked.

"Why not?" Clint replied. "If you want some coffee I'll have to call for another pot."

"No, that's okay. I just wanted to talk."

"Have a seat."

Stoker sat across from Clint.

"How'd you do last night?" Clint asked.

"I came out ahead, a little ahead."

"That's good."

"I just play because I enjoy the game," the policeman said.

"What was it you wanted to talk about?"

"Sam Lance."

"What about him?"

"I looked him up," Stoker said. "Some bad things happened to him five years ago."

"I know that."

"What's he been doing since then?"

"I'm not sure."

"You're his friend, aren't you?"

"New friend."

"How new?"

"I thought I mentioned this yesterday," Clint said. "I met him for the first time in that alley."

"No, you didn't mention that. You said you were in that alley looking for him."

"Oh, well, that was the first time we met."

"But you consider yourself his friend?"

"Well, yeah . . . now."

"So quickly?"

"We spent a lot of time together yesterday," Clint said. "We became friends."

"I see."

"What's this about, Lieutenant?"

"I'm just trying to get the whole story, Mr. Adams," Stoker said. "Mr. Lance used to be a lawman, and had a reputation with a gun."

"So?"

"That is basically your past, too, isn't it?"

"I haven't been a lawman for a long time."

"But the two of you have a reputation with a gun."

"Sam hadn't handled a gun for a long time until yesterday," Clint said.

"When he killed those men."

"Two men," Clint said, "but he only shot one of them."

"Right, he broke the other one's neck."

"Accidentally," Clint said. "What are you trying to find out, here?"

"I guess whether or not Lance is a danger to anyone. I mean, he's a formidable man who's gone on the bottle."

"Drunk he's no danger to anyone."

"And sober?"

"We don't know how long he'll stay sober, but I don't think he's a danger to anyone either way."

"You vouch for him?"

"I do."

"But you've only known him one day."

"Daphne Gibbs will vouch for him," Clint said. "She works for Bat Masterson, and she's known Sam for years."

"I'll talk to her, then. Where is Lance now?"

"He's at The Sportsman's Club. He has a room upstairs. In fact, after today he might have a job there."

"Well," Stoker said, "if he has a job I guess I'd worry about him less."

Stoker stood up. "Will you let me know if he actually gets a job?"

"I will."

"You know," Stoker said, "men like you and Lance attract trouble. Yesterday was a prime example."

"Are you telling me to leave town, Lieutenant?"

"That would be very old-fashioned of me, wouldn't

.. he asked. "Very Dodge City, and Tombstone?"

"Yes, it would be."

"We've come a long way since those days, Mr. Adams," Stoker said. "No, I'm not asking you to leave town, I'm just asking you the same thing I asked you last night."

"Not to kill anyone else."

"Right."

"And the same for Sam Lance?"

"Exactly."

"I'll let him know."

"Fine."

"Hey, Lieutenant."

"Yes?"

"Bat Masterson has the same reputation Sam Lance and I have," Clint said. "Have you had this conversation with him?"

"No."

"Why not?"

"Mr. Masterson is a businessman," Stoker said. " valuable asset to the community."

"I see."

"Also, he's my friend."

"He is?"

"Well, since yesterday. Remember? Any friend of yours is a friend of his?"

"So I guess we're friends too, then?"

Stoker said, "We'll see," and left the dining room.

Clint lifted his cup to his mouth, but his last sip of coffee had gone cold.

What the hell was all that about?

TWENTY-FOUR

Colt James woke up before the whore did. The clerk had been only too happy to send him up a whore after the talk they'd had. Finally unable to sleep because of his hunger Colt decided to substitute sex for food. He'd gone downstairs and asked the clerk if he could find him a whore at this hour.

"A whore's a lot easier than some food at this hour," the man assured him.

"She can't be dirty, or too skinny," Colt said.

"I know just the gal," the clerk assured him.

Colt looked down at the woman now, lying on her stomach with her big breasts crushed beneath her. The clerk had done all right for him, sending him a blonde with meat on her bones. She was no kid, but that was okay with Colt. At thirty-five he didn't mind going ten or fifteen years one way or the other when it came to women. Twenty-five-year-olds had ways of making up for a lack of experience, and forty-five-year-olds certainly had ways of making up for not being young, anymore.

This one had been okay. She was about forty, showing it only on her face some. Her body was still firm, with big tits and wide hips, and a big butt that he had put to good use. She sure didn't mind letting him plug any hole he wanted to, and she had been willing to use her mouth anywhere he wanted her to.

He pulled the sheet down now so he could see her butt. It looked like he had acres and acres of pale flesh in bed with him, which suited him just fine.

He straddled her and rubbed his dick along the crack between her ass cheeks until he was good and hard. She woke up partway through and cooperated by lifting her hips up off the bed. He fingered her until she was good and wet and then slid into her from behind. He plowed her that way for a while, and then when his prick was good and slick from her he withdrew and stuck it in her butt. He got to his knees, she got to hers and he took her that way for a long time, fucking the breath out of her with every thrust of his hips, moving the bed across the floor, making a racket that was sure to wake his brothers. They'd know what he was up to and they'd be lined up outside the door before he finished. This whore was going to have to work a lot harder than she thought she was this morning, but she'd be paid generously for it.

After he exploded with a loud cry she said, "You sure know how to wake a gal up."

"Are you good and awake?" he asked, stepping off the bed and heading for the door.

"Why you ask?" she said, looking over her shoulder. "You mean you ain't done yet, stud?"

"I'm done," he said, opening the door to the hall, "but they ain't even started."

She saw the three men waiting in the hall, eager looks on their faces, wide smiles when they saw her on the bed. Colt was pleased to see that Zeke hadn't gotten there in time and was last in line. The smell wouldn't drive her away, then, before the other two had their turn.

"Friends of yours?" she asked.

"My brothers," he said. "Don't worry. They ain't as big as me, and they don't last long." He looked at his brothers. "Boys, I'm gonna go and find me a bath. Ya'll better be done by the time I get back."

"What about my money?" she asked. "None of these boys looks like they got any."

"I'll pay you when I get back," he said. "Believe me, I got all the stamina in this family, and all the money. You can handle this bunch real easy."

She didn't doubt that. They looked a ragtail group, including the old brother, who wasn't the stud he thought he was. She just hoped he had more money than stamina.

"Okay, then, boys," she said, "the first one of ya step up here, and make sure you close the door behind ya. I ain't puttin' on no sideshow."

When Colt returned from having his bath Danny and Willy were gone, but Zeke was there, snorting and bellowing over the blonde. She had her face buried in the pillow, trying to shield her nose from the smell. Her luck the one who turned out to have the most stamina also had the most body odor.

"That's it, Zeke," Colt said, "you're done."

"Ain't . . . done . . . yet . . ."

"Yeah, well, I can't have ya killin' some whore in my bed," Colt said. He grabbed his brother's shoulder and yanked him out of and off of the blonde whore. Zeke went tumbling to the floor, his erection still wet and prodding the air. "You wanna finish take her to your own room."

"I need to get paid off and outta here, friend," the whore said, getting off the bed and looking for her clothes. "Your brother wants me to go to his room he's gonna have to do two things."

"What's that?"

"Come up with some money of his own," she said, "and take a damned bath first. He always smell like that?"

"It's an affliction," Colt said. He handed the girl some money. She counted it and seemed satisfied.

"You know, there's a little guy hangs out down here on the waterfront a lot. He's about the only one I ever saw smells worse than your brother."

Zeke was there, but they were talking about him like he wasn't.

"You know a lot of the fellas on this waterfront?" Colt asked.

"Most of 'em."

Colt looked at his naked brother and said, "Get up and get out, Zeke. Me and the girl gotta talk."

"I wasn't done!"

"Go take a bath and maybe she'll let ya finish later."

"A bath?" Zeke whined. "Ain't no whore worth takin' a bath!"

Zeke staggered out the door and Colt closed it behind him. He'd been wandering the halls naked, letting the water from his bath dry naturally. Now he turned and looked at the naked whore, money still in her hands.

"We're lookin' for a man," he said, and gave her the same description he'd given the clerk the night before.

"Yeah, he sounds familiar," she said. "He's been on these docks for months, now."

"He ever use you?"

"I never had the pleasure, but then he don't usually have a room and I don't usually work alleys and doorways."

"I know," Colt said, "you got class. Listen, if you see him and let me know, it's worth some money to me."

"I see him you'll be the first to know."

"Thanks."

She looked down at his penis, which had become erect, the two of them standing there naked and all.

"You want me to take care of that for ya?"

"Sure," he said, "while you're here."

She got down on her knees and took him in her mouth. Wouldn't take her long at all.

TWENTY-FIVE

Clint was still wondering what Lieutenant Stoker had really had on his mind that morning as he headed over to Bat's place. The conversation certainly seemed to have been one both men could have done without. After all, what had been accomplished?

It was only four when Clint reached The Sportsman's Club, much earlier than he and Bat had planned the night before. He felt refreshed, though, from the night's sleep he'd had. Also, Sam Lance was no longer his responsibility. He felt relaxed, ready to have something to eat and then to play some poker with men who knew the game.

As he entered he saw that most of the gaming tables were up and running. The two bartenders had business at the bar under control. The young bartender he'd met his first day in town, Cole, smiled as he approached the bar.

"Evenin', Mr. Adams."

"Cole."

"A beer?"

"Thanks."

Cole set the frosty mug on the bar. "On the house, as usual."

"Thanks. Bat around?"

"He's been in and out. He's been talkin' with that fella, that friend of yours, Lance?"

"Sam Lance."

"That's right. I think they're tryin' to settle on a job for him. He an old friend of Bat's, too?"

"A new friend. Actually, Sam is an old friend of Daphne's."

"Ah, Daphne," Cole said, his eyes brightening. "She's my favorite of all the girls."

"That right?"

"I like 'em long and lean like that."

"Does she know?"

"That she's my favorite?" Cole laughed. "Don't think she'd care. I'm just a bartender."

"And she's a saloon girl."

"Oh, she's more than that," Cole said, "much more."

Clint thought Daphne was special, but he had no illusions about her. She was a saloon girl. To Cole, however, she was unattainable. That was his problem. Clint didn't want to take on anybody else's problems, anymore.

"What kind of jobs do you think are available for Sam?" Clint asked.

Cole shrugged and said, "Swamper? He's not a bartender, from the looks of him. And he's not a dealer. And he doesn't wear a gun. I don't know what else he could do."

Lance probably didn't know what else he could do, either.

That morning Bat had invited Sam Lance to breakfast. Over eggs and bacon and potatoes they talked about a job.

"I appreciate your willingness to give me a job, Bat, but—"

"Security."

"What?"

"That's where your talents lie," Bat said. "You were a lawman. I need someone to oversee security."

"I—you don't need a drunk doing that."

"Stop drinking."

"That's easier said than done," Lance said. "You don't know what I see when I close my eyes, Bat."

"I know what I see now, Sam," Bat said. "I see a man in need of a life. Of a reason to live."

"I—I couldn't wear a gun."

"You wouldn't need to," Bat said. "You'd be supervising men who wear guns. I need you to hire them, and oversee them."

"Train them?"

"If need be, but I'd expect you to hire men who didn't need that much training."

Lance sat back and Bat took the opportunity to pour more coffee for both of them.

"You're Bat Masterson," Lance finally said. "Why would you need me to oversee a security force?"

"Because I'm going to be overseeing the gaming operation," Bat said. "I need someone to take care of security, and someone to take care of the dining room."

"Sandy?"

Bat nodded. "She came to work this morning. I'm going to let her completely run the kitchen. She's a good woman, Sam."

"Are you trying to play matchmaker, Bat?"

"I'm just saying."

Lance drank some coffee.

"Let me think about it."

"Sure," Bat said. "No hurry. Keep the room upstairs until you make up your mind. Meanwhile, while you're thinking it over, let me walk you through the whole operation."

Lance thought a moment, then said, "Okay."

When Bat reentered the saloon and gaming area he was alone. He saw Clint at the bar and walked over to him.

"Beer, Bat?" Cole asked.

"Yes, thanks."

"Where's Sam?" Clint asked.

"Taking a walk," Bat said. He accepted his beer from Cole. "I offered him a job."

"Doing what?"

"Security."

"I didn't think of that one," Cole said.

Bat gave him a look and the young man found something to do at the other end of the bar.

"Security," Clint said. "You're taking a risk."

"Probably."

"Why?"

"What happened to him could happen to any of us,"

Bat said. "You, me, Sam, we're alike. I want to help him."

"Did he take the job?"

"He's thinking it over."

"What about Sandy?"

"She showed up this morning," Bat said. "She's going to live upstairs, and be in complete charge of the kitchen."

"Sounds like a big problem solved."

"One, yes."

"What will you do if Sam turns you down?"

"You want to be my partner? Handle security?"

"A partner?" Clint said. "Not a job?"

"No, I offered Sam a job, I'd offer you a partnership."

"I don't think so, Bat," Clint said. "I appreciate the offer, but no. I don't need a job or a partnership."

"Then I hope Sam takes the job."

"He'll have to stay off the whiskey."

"That's gonna be his decision," Bat said. "If he does, then he'll be able to do the job. If not . . ." Bat just shrugged.

"When will he give you his answer?"

"Next couple of days," Bat said. "Meanwhile, we can play some poker."

"I'm ready."

"Ready to sample my new kitchen first?"

Clint put his beer mug down on the bar. "Lead the way."

Bat set his mug down next to Clint's. "I understand she makes a mean stew, too."

"Let's go and find out how good."

TWENTY-SIX

Sandy came out to their table after they had eaten their stew and were starting on their pie. Throughout the dining room Bat could see satisfied diners, and he was happy.

"How was your dinner?" she asked.

"Excellent!" Bat said. "Delicious. I can't think of enough superlatives."

"Clint?"

"Great stew," Clint said, "great pie."

"I now have the best kitchen in Denver," Bat said.

"Well, I don't know," Sandy said. "I heard the kitchen at the Palace is pretty good."

"I've eaten at the Palace," Bat said. He looked at Clint. "I had to sample the competition."

"And?"

"The food was very good." He looked at Sandy. "Your food is better. No, not only better, it's much better."

"I'm flattered."

"See this dining room?" Bat said. "Every other table

131

is empty. When the word gets out that I finally have a good cook—a great cook—it'll be full every night."

"I'll need help in the kitchen, then," Sandy said.

"You'll get it," Bat said. "Hire all the help you need, as long as the food always tastes like you made it."

Sandy shook her head and said, "I really can't believe this. It's all happened so fast."

"Believe it," Bat said. "And when I finally buy the Palace I'll take you with me."

"I better get back to the kitchen before I swoon," she said.

"You know," Bat said, "she'd be real good for Sam."

"They're friends."

"They could be more."

"Not as long as he blames himself for his wife's death," Clint observed.

"Maybe she can help him get over it."

"Let's talk about the Palace," Clint said. "Who's going to be playing tonight?"

"Well, for one, Ed Chase, one of the owners of the place. Have you ever been there?"

"Never."

"It's all brick, on the corner of Blake and Fifteenth. They call it The Palace Theater but I've already got my own name picked out for it."

"What's that?"

" 'The Palace Variety Theater and Gambling Parlors,' " Bat recited. "See, they got more than one room inside for gambling."

"Bat, I'd think you'd want to hang onto your own place."

"Hey, this place is an investment, so I can buy that one."

"What makes you think they'll sell?"

"Everybody sells, sooner or later," Bat said. "The same goes for Ed Chase and Ed Gaylord—the two Eds, I call 'em."

"What's the reputation of the place?"

"A place for square gambling," Bat said, "but that don't keep people from trying to close it down. Reverend Henry Martin Hart—the 'Very' Reverend—called it 'a death trap to young men and a foul den of vice and corruption.' You can't buy that kind of publicity."

"I guess not. When do you expect to be able to buy it?"

"Two years," Bat said. "That's my game plan."

"And who knows about this plan?"

"You."

"Nobody else?"

"Nobody."

"You have any partners in this place, Bat?" Clint asked. "Any silent partners?"

"Not a one. It's all mine."

"Well, that's good," Clint said. "There won't be any complications there."

Bat sat back and lit up a cigar. "I got this planned to a fair thee well Clint. Nothin' can go wrong."

"Not as long as gambling is legal."

"Don't say things like that," Bat scolded him. "Gamblin' will always be legal."

Clint wasn't so sure about that, but he decided not to

argue the point with his friend. Bat was in too good a mood.

Clint took a look over Bat's shoulder and noticed Sam Lance approaching the table.

"Here comes Sam."

Bat didn't turn. "Think he's made up his mind already?"

"He looks pretty determined."

"I hope he takes the job," Bat said. "That'll mean I took care of two problems in one day."

"That'd make you pretty lucky."

"Then all I'd need is a good run of luck at the tables tonight to top it all off."

"Ed Chase any good?"

"He's a pretty good card player, for a square gambler."

"Well, Sam looks like a man with his mind made up," Clint said. "My bet would be he's taking the job."

"Well," Bat said, "I'm not going to bet against you, because that's just what I want to hear."

TWENTY-SEVEN

"They told me at the bar I'd find you here," Lance said to Bat when he reached the table. "Hello, Clint."

"Sam."

"This crazy man tell you the job he offered me?"

"He told me."

"Have a seat, Sam," Bat said. "Some coffee?"

"Yeah, coffee's fine."

There was already an extra cup on the table so Bat poured Lance his coffee.

"Have you got an answer for me already?"

"I do," Lance said. "If the job is still open, I'll take it."

"It's open," Bat said, "and it's yours. When can you start?"

"Tomorrow," Lance said. "I'm gonna need a few things, though."

"Like what?"

"Like clothes, for one thing, and a place of my own."

"You're my security chief," Bat said. "Your place is here. The room you got suit you?"

135

"It does."

"Then I'll advance you some money and you can get yourself some clothes tomorrow . . . and anything else you might need."

"I won't carry a gun."

"I'm not askin' you to."

"But I'm gonna buy a billy club."

"Whatever you want to arm yourself with is your business," Bat said, "as long as you don't use it on my high rollers."

"Only if they break the rules."

"I guess we'll have to work on those rules together."

"I got no objection to that."

"All right, then," Bat said, extending his hand. "We got a deal."

Lance accepted the hand and said, "We've got a deal."

"Guess I'm a witness," Clint said.

"You're more than that," Lance said. "You're the one I have to thank."

"Actually," Bat said, "the same goes for me."

"Oh no," Clint said, "you fellas worked this little deal out yourselves. If it doesn't work I don't want the blame."

"Oh, it'll work out," Bat said. "Right, Sam?"

Lance hesitated, thinking about Dulcy, and a bottle of whiskey, but finally he said, "Right, Bat."

TWENTY-EIGHT

Clint and Bat went right from dinner to The Palace Theater. When they arrived Clint could see from the outside why Bat wanted it. You could have fit Bat's Sportsman's Club inside with room left over. Once Bat had the Palace, he would be the premier gambler and sportsman in Denver.

They entered and Bat took some time to give Clint a tour. He showed him the actual theater, where musicals were put on, and where Lillie Langtry herself had once performed. Clint had met Lillie Langtry in New York some time ago and the two had gotten along very well.

The gambling rooms were huge, with very little elbow room to be had at the tables or at the bar. The ceiling was very high, with crystal chandeliers hanging down. The smell of clean leather was heavy in the air, as the huge bar was lined with red leather.

Bat took Clint to the smoking room, the dining room, and the lounge, and then back to the main hall.

"What do you think?"

"You're going to have enough money to buy this place in just two years?"

"That's the plan."

"I wish you luck," Clint said. "This place is amazing."

"Here comes our host."

Clint turned to see a dapper man in a black suit and black boots with a high, blinding shine. He had all the earmarks of a gambler, and strongly resembled their friend Luke Short.

"Bat, so good to see you," Ed Chase said. He extended his hand and shook Bat's warmly. "And is this Mr. Adams?"

"It is," Bat said. "Clint, meet Ed Chase, the owner of the Palace."

"Co-owner," Ed Chase said, shaking Clint's hand as warmly as he had Bat's. "It's a great pleasure to have you at the Palace, Mr. Adams. Your reputation precedes you."

"I'm almost afraid to ask which reputation that is, Mr. Chase."

"Please, call me Ed," Chase said, "and the reputations I know of are as a gentleman and a poker player."

"Hmm," Clint said, "I don't know who you've been listening to, then."

"Why, Bat, of course," Chase said. "Has he given you the tour?"

"Yes," Clint said, "I can't tell you how impressed I am. You've got quite a place here."

"We have, indeed," Chase said. "My partner, Ed Gaylord, and I are very proud. You'll get to meet Ed later."

"Will he be playing?"

"I'm afraid I'm the Ed who gambles," Chase said. "Ed makes sure I don't lose all of our profits."

"So who would be at the game?"

Chase smiled and said, "Several of our most prominent citizens who have the money and the inclination to gamble, as well as any of the top sportsmen in the country who are in Denver." Chase turned to Bat. "Did you tell him about the fight?"

"No, not yet."

"A fight?"

"We'll have a prizefight here in a couple of nights, a couple of heavyweight contenders trying to make names for themselves. That should bring several more sportsmen to town, as well."

"Well, it sounds like it could be an interesting night."

"Two tables," Ed Chase said, "six men to a table. Twelve very coveted chairs, and only the best—or richest—players will be allowed in."

"Well, I'm not rich, so I think I might be getting in under false pretenses."

"Bat vouches for you," Ed Chase said. "That's all you need to qualify. Why don't the two of you make yourselves at home, have a drink, sit in the lounge, or have a cigar. I'll be along to fetch you for the game a little later. I just have to check on the room, and the other players."

"Thank you, Ed," Clint said.

Chase shook hands with both of them and walked off to take care of business.

"He seems very much in control."

"He's a wild man at the table," Bat said. "Hardly ever

folds, throws good money after bad. We can make a lot of money just off of him."

"Do you know who else will be playing?"

"I have an idea about a few of the men, but you never know who's in town and who will show up."

"Luke's not in town, is he?" Clint asked.

"No," Bat said, "I'd know if he was. Also, Ben Thompson's not around, and neither are Bret, Bart, or Brady."

They had just named the five gamblers they would have been most concerned about playing. Other than those five, there were no likely surprises.

"So what will you have?" Bat asked. "Drink or cigar?"

"Drink, I think."

"Let's go to the lounge and have it brought to us," Bat suggested. "The service here is impeccable."

They walked toward the lounge and Bat said, "There are a few changes I would make when I buy the place, but for the most part I'd let it run just the way it does now."

"Really?" Clint asked. "What changes would you make?"

"Let's wait until we're seated and we have our drinks," Bat said, "and I'll bounce a few ideas off of you and see what you think."

Ed Chase made his way to his private office, just down the hall from his partner's. No sooner had he entered than there was a knock at his door.

"Come in, Ed," he said. He barely had time to seat

himself behind his desk when his partner walked in.

"Is Bat here with Adams?" Gaylord asked.

"They're both here," Chase said.

"Did you talk to them?"

"No," Chase said, "not yet."

"Why not?"

"It wasn't the time, Ed."

"When will be the time, Ed?"

Gaylord was the same age as Chase, late forties, early fifties, but he was a much larger man. They went to the same tailor, but while Ed Chase's suits always looked perfectly fitted, Ed Gaylord's suits always hung on him like they were the wrong size.

"Relax, Ed," Chase said. "Let me get them involved in the game for a while, before I hit them up."

"Just make sure you don't get so involved in the game that you forget," Gaylord said, "and so you don't lose a fortune of our money."

"Don't worry, Ed," Chase said. "I know what I'm doing around a card table."

"Oh sure," Gaylord said, "It's only when there's money on the table that you have a hard time."

TWENTY-NINE

"See, they've got waiters bringing us our drinks here," Bat said. "That's because it's a men's-only lounge."

"And what would you do?" Clint asked. "Allow women in?"

"Oh no," Bat said, "but I would have waitresses instead of waiters."

"Bat," Clint said, "a waitress is a woman."

"I know that."

"If you have waitresses, then it's not men only, anymore."

"Waitresses can come in and serve drinks to *men only*," Bat said. "It'll still be only men who can come in here and relax. They'll just have something pretty to look at while they're doing it."

"I see."

"Don't tell me you don't like looking at pretty girls while you drink," Bat said.

"I love looking at pretty girls," Clint said, supporting his friend's idea. "I think it's a great idea."

"Good," Bat said. "I knew you would."

"What other changes do you have in mind?"

Bat was sitting with a brandy while Clint had a beer. Bat was holding a walking stick, and had set his bowler on top of it. Clint always thought walking sticks were for people with bad legs, but Bat simply liked to carry one from time to time and—more than once—Clint had seen Bat use it to save his life, or someone else's. Bat also made it work as a fashion statement. Clint knew few men who dressed better—or as well—as Bat Masterson.

"The men who come in here are going to have to dress better," Bat said.

"What?"

"Look at them," Bat said. "There isn't a man in here who wouldn't benefit from a visit to my tailor."

"Including me?"

"You, my friend," Bat said, "have a style all your own."

Clint wasn't at all sure that this was a compliment.

"So let me get this straight," Clint said. "The men are going to have to dress better, but you're going to have half-naked waitresses working here. Do I have that right?"

"Exactly right," Bat said. "What do you think?"

Clint groped for the right word, then just settled for "Perfect!"

"I knew you'd back me," Bat said, beaming.

They were still discussing possible changes when Ed Chase came to the lounge to get them.

"Have you been well taken care of?" Chase asked.

"The service has been excellent," Clint said.

"We are a little anxious to start taking some of your money, though, Ed," Bat said.

"Confident as ever, Bat," Chase said, clapping Bat on the shoulder.

"Mr. Chase?"

Chase turned and faced a man wearing a tuxedo.

"Gentlemen, my head waiter, Rick."

Rick nodded at Clint and Bat and then said to Chase, "I need to speak to you about something . . . in private?"

Chase turned to Bat and Clint. "A little business. Just let me take care of it and then we'll go up."

"Up?" Clint asked as Chase walked away with Rick.

"Private room," Bat said. "He's feeling cocky, confident. That's good."

"How can you tell?"

"The way he slapped me on the back?" Bat said. "Very patronizing. Good ol' Bat, as confident as ever. He thinks he's going to take us."

"Well, I hope we sit at the table he's sitting at," Clint said.

"I have an idea about that."

"What?"

"Why should we bother to butt heads with each other?" Bat suggested.

"You're suggesting we sit at separate tables?"

"We can both make out that way."

"And which one of us gets to sit with Chase?"

Bat smiled. "I've played with Ed before, so I'll leave him to you. I'll make the suggestion to him. I know he'll want to play against you."

"Hey, if you can make it happen, go ahead," Clint said, "but I know what you're really doing."

"What's that?"

"You just don't want to play against me."

"Yes," Bat said, patting Clint on the shoulder in exactly the same manner Ed Chase had patted his shoulder just a short time ago, "that's it exactly."

On the way up to the private room Bat took hold of Ed Chase's arm and walked him a little ahead of Clint. He whispered in Chase's ear, then looked back at Clint and nodded. The seating arrangements were apparently all set.

Now it was time to play.

THIRTY

The James Brothers—not to be confused with the "James Boys"—worked the waterfront for most of the day, splitting up and looking for Sam Lance who, five years ago, had killed their brother Steve in a gunfight. They were aware that Lance's wife had also been killed that day, but did not feel that this was proper punishment for the killing of their brother.

They split up, Colt going his way with Zeke, and Willy and Danny staying together. After they had come up empty they met at a small saloon a few blocks from their hotel, which also served food. They settled for sandwiches and beer.

"Tell us again how we know he's even here," Willy said to Colt.

"I told you," Colt said. "I got a telegram saying that Sam Lance had been seen on the waterfront in Denver."

"That's all?" Danny said.

"That's it."

"Well he sure wasn't here today," Zeke said.

"Maybe he was," Colt said, "but your smell drove him away."

"Aw, Colt—"

"Shut up," Colt said to Zeke. He addressed all three brothers. "We'll go out again tomorrow and keep looking."

"What about the rest of tonight?" Danny asked.

"You boys can do whatever you want tonight."

Danny's eyes lit up. "I wanna check out Bat Masterson's new place I heard about."

"The Sportsman's Club," Willy said, "I heard about it, too."

"You wanna come, Colt?" Danny asked.

"No," Colt said. "I'll stick around here."

Danny and Willy stood up, neither of them asking brother Zeke if he wanted to go. Zeke watched as they left, on their way to do some gambling.

"We're the two older brothers, Colt," Zeke said. "They should treat us with more respect."

"They treat me with plenty of respect, Zeke," Colt said. "Besides, Steve and me was the older brothers. You're the middle brother."

Zeke always hated being the middle brother. His big secret in life was that he hadn't been so disappointed when brother Steve had been killed. He thought it would mean that he wasn't the middle brother, anymore. Obviously, that was not the case.

"Colt, what are you gonna do tonight?"

"I don't know."

"I wanna find that blonde whore from this morning," Zeke said. "I didn't get ta finish. What was her name?"

"I forget."

"Come on," Zeke said, "How'm I gonna find her if I don't know her name?"

"Go and ask the desk clerk what her name was," Colt said. "He's the one who got her for me. He can send her to your room for you."

"That's a good idea," Zeke said, standing up. "I'm gonna go do that right now."

"Good," Colt said. "I could use some time alone."

"I'll see you later."

"Tomorrow," Colt said. "We don't have to see each other until tomorrow."

"Okay," Zeke said, "tomorrow."

Colt didn't even watch as Zeke left. Suddenly, with Zeke out of his face and his other brothers off gambling, he felt at ease. He went to the bar and got himself another beer.

"I hear you're lookin' for Sam Lance," the bartender said, as he set the beer down.

"I might be. What's it to you?"

"Might be I could help ya."

"You know where Lance is?"

"No," the barkeep said, "but I might know somebody who does."

"Who?"

The bartender did not reply. Colt sipped his beer and stared at the man, who stared back. Eventually, however, the barman averted his eyes, not liking what he saw in the eyes of Colton James.

"Well," he said, "I could help ya out and you kin pay me later, if the information pans out."

"What's the information?"

"He's got a friend who never leaves the waterfront."

"Name?"

"Billy Drew."

"How will I know him?"

"Little guy, smells real bad."

"Friend," Colt said, "I got a brother who smells real bad. That ain't gonna help me."

"No," the bartender said, "Billy smells real bad—and the more nervous he gets, the worse the smell gets. Around here they call him Smelly Billy."

"Where do I find Smelly Billy?"

"Well," the barman said, "could be if you sat around here long enough he'd come in lookin' for a free drink."

"He come in every night?"

"Most nights," the barman said. "The Wayfarer Saloon is his favorite."

"Well, then," Colt said, "I guess I'll sit around here for a while and see if he shows up. He walks in you give me the high sign, you hear?"

"I hear."

"And if he can help me out," James said, "it'll be worth somethin' to ya."

"Fair enough."

"If you're wastin' my time, it'll be worth your time to find a new job."

"Hey, I own this place."

"If you're wastin' my time," Colt said, "I'd think about sellin' it if I was you."

He took his beer and walked back to his table. The bartender bit his lip and hoped Billy Drew would come walking through the door . . . soon!

THIRTY-ONE

To Clint's disappointment there were no players of note in the room by the time everyone had arrived. However, that did not mean that there were no good players in the game. That would remain to be seen once the play began.

The players seemed to be split between local businessmen who enjoyed playing with professional gamblers, and professional gamblers who were in town. It was not a special "invitation" game, or there would have been some gamblers of note there. As it was Clint recognized the names of some of the gamblers, but did not think they were in the league of, say, a Bat Masterson.

As Bat had promised, Clint sat at a table with Ed Chase. Also at the table was another professional gambler and three local businessmen. The split at Bat's table was three gamblers, three businessmen. Clint assumed that Chase was considering himself and Clint among the pros. He quickly learned that Bat had been dead-on about Ed Chase's play. The man stayed in too many hands to ever be a good poker player.

Actually, two of the other players were local businessmen, and one was a politician. None of the three was particularly skillful, though, so Clint's only competition at the table was a gambler named Timothy Burroughs.

After a few hours both Clint and Burroughs were up while the rest of the table was losing. Clint found it unusual that Chase would be playing a game where the deal passed from hand to hand, rather than using his house dealers. He sneaked a glance over to the other table and saw that Bat had an impressive stack of chips in front of him. The plan to play at separate tables was paying off for both of them.

At the Wayfarer Saloon Colt James was nursing a second mug of beer for so long it had gone warm. He was trying to decide whether to get another, or just leave when the bartender looked over at him and gave him a high sign. The front doors had just opened and a small man stepped through.

"How about a drink, Tor?" Billy Drew whined. "I got an awful bad thirst."

"You got any money, Billy?" Tor asked.

"I'll pay ya tomorrow, I swear."

"Forget it, Billy," Tor said. "You ain't gettin' a drink here unless somebody buys it for ya."

Sadly, Billy looked around at the few men who were in the saloon. Most were ignoring him, but one spoke up.

"Hey, little man," Colt said, "I'll buy you a beer."

"Much obliged, mister."

"Give the man a beer, bartender."

"Sure thing."

Tor set a beer in front of Billy, who reached for it thirstily. Before he could close his hand over it, though, someone else's hand came over his shoulder and grabbed it.

"Come on over here and have it with me," Colt said.

"Uh, sure, sure thing, mister."

Billy followed Colt to his table and sat down. Colt set the beer in front of him and inhaled. The bartender had been right about the little man's smell, but Colt's experience with his own brother's body odors enabled him to handle it. He sat across from Billy and watched him drink down half his beer greedily, as if he thought Colt might change his mind and take it away from him.

"Good?" Colt asked.

"Sure is, mister," Billy said, wiping his mouth on his sleeve. "Thanks."

"Well, now that you drank half of it you got to earn the other half." Colt reached out and drew the half-filled mug out of Billy's reach. The little man looked as if he might cry.

"W-what do I gotta do?"

"It's simple," Colt said. "All ya gotta do is answer one question."

Suspiciously, Billy asked, "What question?"

"Where's Sam Lance?"

Billy Drew's heart sank, and his body gave off the sorriest stench of fear.

●　　●　　●

Willy and Danny James were each indulging in their greatest passions at Bat Masterson's Sportsman's Club. Willy was playing blackjack and Danny was playing roulette. Danny couldn't play blackjack because he couldn't remember which cards were good. With roulette, all he had to do was pick a number and put a chip on it, and Danny always played the same number—thirteen. It was his lucky number. He'd already hit it three times, and if he had been betting more than a dollar at a time he would have been doing pretty good.

Willy was also doing well, but was also only betting a dollar a hand. Both men thought a dollar was a lot of money to bet, and had no idea that anyone was betting more, because they didn't pay attention to anyone else's play. So neither knew that they were the joke of the tables they were playing at.

Carl Evert was watching both tables carefully. The two men who resembled each other seemed to be doing well, but they were betting so little that the other men at the tables were laughing at them. They didn't seem to notice, but he was afraid that if and when they did there would be trouble.

The Sportsman's Club didn't have a security force yet, but Evert knew that Bat had just hired Sam Lance for that.

Evert called over one of the girls, a redhead named Gina and said, "Go upstairs and ask Mr. Lance if he'll come down, will you, doll?"

"Sure, Carl."

"Tell him I know he doesn't start until tomorrow, but

there's a situation down here he could help me with."

"Sure, Carl."

"Thank you, sweetie."

Gina was sleeping with Carl, and was willing to do anything he asked of her. This was an easy errand to perform. She rather enjoyed some of the harder things he asked her to do, when they were in bed.

Sam Lance had taken his advance from Bat and gone shopping earlier in the day. He had a couple of suits, a new hat, and a billy club that he was going to carry when he was on duty. Daphne and Clint, and Bat too, had been so good to him that he was determined to make this job work, even though at the moment he was desperate for a drink. He was thinking about Dulcy, and a bottle of whiskey, when there was a knock on his door.

THIRTY-TWO

"Hi, I'm Gina," the girl at the door said.

"Hi."

"Are you, um, Sam?"

"That's right." He recognized the girl from downstairs, but couldn't imagine what she'd want with him. "Can I help you?"

"Carl sent me up? Carl Evert?"

Lance had met Evert during his tour of the place with Bat, so he knew who the man was.

"I know Mr. Evert," Lance said.

"Well, he told me to tell you that he knows you don't start until tomorrow, but if you could come down now you could help with a, uh, situation."

Lance turned around and looked at his new suits, his hat, and the billy club on the bed, then looked at the girl again. She was a little on the plump side, very pretty, and young, probably no more than twenty-three or -four. He doubted she knew who he was other than what Carl Evert might have told her.

"Well," he said to her, "I don't see any reason I can't

come downstairs and start my new job tonight, do you?"

"Are you gonna be working here?" she asked.

"I'm the new head of security."

"I didn't know we had any security."

He smiled and said, "Well, that's going to be one of my jobs. Okay, then, let's go down—oh, wait a minute."

He went to the bed and picked up his club. He still hadn't decided how he would carry it, but for now he'd just keep it in his hand.

"Let's go."

"Aren't you going to wear a gun?" she asked. "I mean, if you're in charge of security, and all?"

"No," Lance said, "I'm not gonna wear a gun."

"Wow," she said, impressed, "then you must be really good at your job."

"I guess that's what we're gonna find out, aren't we?"

"W-what?" Billy Drew asked.

"You heard me," Colt James said. "Where can I find Sam Lance? I know he's on this waterfront."

Whew! The odor coming from the little man was starting to make his eyes water. He was going to have to start taking it easy on Zeke, whose body odor had never been quite this bad. This smelly little man must have been very afraid.

"You do know Sam Lance, don't you?" Colt asked.

"Uh, oh, yeah, sure, Sam," Billy said. "I knew him."

"Knew him?"

"When he was here."

"He's not here anymore?"

"Nope," Billy said, shaking his head. In point of fact,

he had not seen Sam Lance since the shooting in the alley. He'd gone back later to retrieve the bottle of whiskey, but Lance had never come back to the alley.

"He's gone."

"Gone where?"

"I don't know."

"Were you friends?"

"We was real good friends," Billy said, before he realized it. "Sometimes we even shared a bottle." He shut up, then, realizing he might have said too much.

"So, if you and Sam were good friends, he wouldn't leave town without sayin' good-bye, would he?"

"Oh, um, yeah, probably," Billy said.

"Why's that?"

"He made a new friend."

"And who was that."

"Fella named, uh, Adams."

"This Adams got a first name?" Colt asked. He moved the beer mug around on the table, sort of dangling it in front of the man.

"Clint," Billy said, "Clint Adams."

He reached for the mug, grabbed it and brought it to his mouth. He knew he had to drink it down before the man changed his mind and took it away from him.

"Clint Adams?" Colt James repeated. "You mean . . . the Gunsmith? That Clint Adams?"

"Yup," Billy said, pushing the empty mug away. He felt real proud to have gotten it all down—so proud that maybe he got a little cocky. "Mister Adams is my friend, too. We killed us some men together."

"You did, huh?"

"Yessiree."

"Where did this happen?"

"In an alley not far from here," Billy said. "Me, Clint, and Sam."

"Sam Lance killed a man?"

"Two," Billy said, proudly. "Shot one, and broke the other's neck."

Colt had been under the impression that Lance was a washed-up drunk, an easy target for him and his brothers. Now he was hearing that not only had Lance killed two men, but he had teamed himself up with the Gunsmith.

"Billy," Colt said, "is all of this true?"

"Sure, it's true!" Billy said. "I ain't no liar."

"Would you lie for a bottle of whiskey?"

"A bottle?" Billy asked, his eyes widening. "A whole bottle?"

"A whole bottle."

Billy touched his lips, which had suddenly gone dry.

"Lie about what?"

"I'll give you a bottle of whiskey," Colt said. "All you got to do is tell me whether or not you're telling the truth."

"The truth?"

Colt nodded.

"I got to believe you, Billy," Colt said. "If I find out you were lying to me, I'd have to come back and hurt you."

"Hurt—"

"Hurt you bad, me and my three brothers."

Billy frowned. "I'm confused," he complained, and the smell got even worse.

"Bring me a bottle!" Colt shouted to the bartender.

Tor came around the bar with a bottle of the vilest rotgut he had on his shelf. It was good enough for Billy. It'd do the trick for him if it didn't make him go blind, or kill him.

Colt took the bottle and held it in front of Billy. Tor went back behind the bar.

"Simple question, Billy," he said. "Did Sam Lance really kill two men in an alley with Clint Adams?"

"Well," Billy said, slowly, "Clint killed two and Sam killed two. Wait . . . yeah, there was four, and they killed them two each."

"And you didn't kill anyone?"

Billy pouted. "No," he said, "that was a lie."

Colt studied the stinky little man and decided he believed him.

"Where do you think Sam went, Billy?"

"With Clint Adams," Billy said, morosely. "They left together."

"Because they're friends now?"

"Yeah."

"And neither of them is friends with you, anymore?"

"That's right," Billy said. Suddenly, he was feeling hurt, and a little angry. "Yeah, that's right. They both left me."

"Now, this last question is real important, Billy, and then you get the bottle."

"Okay."

"Where do you think they went?"

Billy thought for a moment, then screwed up his face and looked like he was going to cry.

"I don't know where they went," he said, mournfully. "Can't I have the bottle?"

"Think, Billy," Colt said. "Think hard. Maybe one of them said something, maybe you can make a guess. I'll take a guess from you."

Billy thought some more, started to squeeze big tears from his eyes. He was crying because his friend had left him, and he was crying because he wanted the bottle this man was holding, so bad.

And then it hit him.

"Wait!"

"What is it? Did you remember something?"

"Bat Masterson!"

"What?"

"Clint mentioned Bat Masterson."

"Masterson is in Denver, too?" Colt asked.

From the bar Tor said, "He's got hisself a new gambling place called The Sportsman's Club. Any driver could take ya there."

"Adams," Colt said to himself, "and Masterson, and Sam Lance."

This was starting to sound like it wasn't going to be as easy as they'd thought.

"Mister?" Billy asked. "Could I have the bottle?"

Colt looked at the bottle in his hand. He could see how cheap the stuff was. He sure didn't want it, so he held it out to Billy, who grabbed it with both hands.

"Drink yerself into a stupor, Billy," he said. "Drink yerself to death."

"Thank you, mister," Billy said. "Thanks a lot."

THIRTY-THREE

The game broke for fifteen minutes, giving Clint and Bat time to have a drink together and compare notes.

"I'm killin' 'em," Bat said. "I'm the only one winning at my table."

"I've got a little competition at my table from a fella named Tim Burroughs."

"I know the name," Bat said. "He's young, been making a little bit of a name for himself in private games. Heard he went head to head with Ben last month and came out ahead."

"You go head to head with Ben Thompson and come out alive you're ahead," Clint observed.

"Ben's okay," Bat said. "A little bit of a hothead."

"You and Ben don't get along."

"I know," Bat said. "I was just tryin' to be nice."

"You were right about Ed Chase, by the way," Clint said. "He's throwing good money after bad."

"I know it!" Bat said. "I'm damned glad he's not my partner. Poor Ed Gaylord."

"Time's up," Ed Chase called out. "Has anyone

dropped out, or does anyone have to leave?"

Two players dropped out from Bat's table because they tapped out, and the two businessmen at Clint's table left because they had to work in the morning. That left four players at each table.

"We can play a table of eight if everyone agrees to five card stud," Chase said. "Anyone object?"

The remaining players all exchanged glances and no one objected. To that point three games had been popular at all three tables: five stud, seven stud, and draw. Now they'd all be playing five card stud.

"Just give me a few moments to consolidate the tables," Ed Chase said, "and we can start up again."

"I love five card stud," Bat said.

"I kind of like draw," Clint said, "but stud's okay."

"What's your man Burroughs's game?"

"He's been dealing seven stud."

"This should be interesting," Bat said. He looked at Clint and raised the remainder of his drink in a toast. "Every man for himself?"

"Every man for himself."

"And no hard feelings."

"None."

"Yep," Bat said, "now it gets interesting."

Sam Lance followed Gina down the stairs and across the gaming floor to where Carl Evert was standing.

"Thanks, Gina," Evert said. "You can go back to work now."

She gave Evert a radiant smile and flounced off.

"Problems?" Lance asked.

"Potential problems," Evert said. "I know you haven't started yet, but—"

"What's it about?"

"From here you can see both tables, roulette and blackjack." Evert described the two men and waited until Lance was sure he knew who they were.

"Okay, I got 'em," Lance said. "What's the problem?"

Evert explained about the table limits, and how the two men were playing the very bottom. This, he told Lance, was going to get them ribbed in about ten minutes.

"If I'm any judge," Evert added. "The others have been watching them for half an hour, and they're all about ready to bust."

"You know the other men at the tables?"

"I do," Evert said. "The ribbing will be good-natured, but if I'm any judge of character these two are not going to take it well."

"Okay," Lance said. "I'll keep my eye on them. You got other work to do?"

"Yes."

"Then you can go do it."

"You can handle this?"

"Sure."

Evert studied Lance for a moment.

"You, uh, don't have a gun."

"You want anybody killed over this?"

"God, no! Bat would kill me."

"Then I should be able to handle it with this." Lance showed Evert his club.

"Well, all right," Evert said, finally. "If you need help

all you'll have to do is call on the dealers."

"They're job is dealin'," Lance said. "Security is mine. Don't worry."

"I won't," Evert said. "Bat wouldn't have hired you if you weren't good."

Evert moved away and Lance moved over to where he could watch both tables closely. After a few moments he could see what Evert was referring to. Some of the other players were already nudging each other and whispering. Pretty soon the laughter would start out loud.

He felt a trembling in his stomach. He wasn't half as confident as he had let Evert think, but nevertheless this was something he was going to have to handle himself. If he couldn't diffuse this situation, then there was no way he was going to be able to do this job.

THIRTY-FOUR

It started at the roulette table.

"Wow, cowboy," one of the players said, "you gonna start makin' some big bets soon?"

Danny looked up to see who was speaking, and to whom they were speaking, and found everybody looking at him.

"You talkin' to me?" he asked.

"That's right," the spokesman said. "How about betting some real money here? Or else you're takin' up a space somebody who really wants to play can use."

Danny laughed and said, "Hey, friend, I'm bettin' a whole dollar at a time. What are you bettin'?"

" 'A whole dollar at a time,' " the spokesman, a cowboy himself by the looks of him, said. "Friend, I'm bettin' five and ten dollars number, and I'm playin' more than one number."

"That's probably why yer losin'," Danny said. "And you can't be bettin' no five dollars. That's a lot of money."

"You ever played in a casino before, friend?" the cow-

poke asked. "They got these games where you come
from?"

"We got us a wheel where I come from," Danny said.
"Some of the boys bets quarters and half-dollars, but I'm
considered a high roller 'cause I bet whole dollars."

" 'Whole dollars,' " the cowpoke said, quoting Danny
again, and then he started laughing. Pretty soon the
whole table was laughing and Danny was lookin' real
hurt.

At the blackjack table Willy looked over at the roulette
table to see what was so funny.

"That your brother over there, friend?" one of the
other players asked. "The one bettin' whole dollars."

Willy looked at the man who was speaking.

"We both bet dollars, friend," he said. "That too steep
for ya?"

"Too steep?" the man asked, and started laughing.
Soon both tables were laughing out loud at both brothers.

"Ya shouldn't oughtta be laughin'," Danny said.

Willy, slightly more levelheaded than Danny, saw that
his brother was going to reach for his gun.

"Danny, don't!"

Too late. Danny went for the gun and Willy knew
he'd have to back his brother's play.

"Hold on, friend," Sam Lance said. He stepped in
close to Danny and jammed his hand down on the man's
gunhand. Try as he might, Danny couldn't get his gun
out of his holster.

"Mister," Willy said, stepping over to the roulette table, "that's my brother."

"I know it," Lance said. "Ease up on your gun, too, friend."

"Let go of my brother, before I—" Willy started to draw his gun and, using his free hand and his club, Lance brought the weapon down on Willy's wrist. He struck the protruding bone in the wrist and Willy's whole hand went dead as he howled. As he turned to put his hand between his legs to hold it Lance was able to drop his club and grab Willy's gun from his holster. At the same time he released Danny's hand, but before the man could move he had his gun, too.

"Catch!" he called out, and tossed one gun each to the two dealers, who managed to catch them. Lance bent and retrieved his club, then faced the two brothers.

"You broke my wrist!" Willy shouted.

"You had no call ta do that, mister," Danny complained. "They was laughin' at us."

"It was good clean fun, friend," Lance said. "No need for gunplay, at all."

"Says you."

"Well, I'm the law in this saloon," Lance said, "so I guess you're right, says me."

"Goddamn!" Willy swore. "Broke my wrist!"

"It's not broke," Lance said, "but it'll be a might sore for a while." He looked at Danny. "Why don't you take your brother out of here and see to him?"

"We got money on the tables, mister," Danny said.

"I'll have somebody meet you at the front door with

your money, and with your guns—unloaded. If you load them and come back in, you'll be sorry."

"You ain't got no gun," Danny said, "just that club."

"It was all I needed, this time, wasn't it?"

Danny fumed and glared at Lance.

"Besides, your brother isn't gonna be able to use that hand for a while," Lance said. "Go on, take him out and take care of him."

"Can I help?" Carl Evert asked, appearing at Lance's side.

"Cash these boys out, Carl, and see that their money is taken to the door along with their unloaded guns. They've decided to leave."

"Okay, Sam." Evert looked at the two dealers. "You heard him."

Danny helped Willy to the door, people who had been crowded around now moving away to form a path for them. The dealers met them at the door, gave them their money and slid their empty guns into their holsters.

"Don't come back," one of the dealers said.

Danny stared at them and said, "We'll see you again."

"Not smart," the other dealer said.

Willy glared at them, and then past them to Lance.

"I'll see him again," he said. "Me and my brothers."

"Not a good idea," the first dealer said. "That's Sam Lance."

"What?" Danny said.

"Marshal Sam Lance? From Kingdom? He was a hell-uva lawman in his day. Now he's hired on here as head of security."

"So don't come back," the other man said. "Now get!"

Danny grabbed Willy's arm and tugged him outside.

Out on the street he said to Willy, "Did you hear that?"

"I didn't hear nothin' " Willy said. "My damn arm is—"

"That fella with the club, Willy," Danny said. "It was Sam Lance."

"The hell you say!"

"That's what them dealers said," Danny said. "Sam Lance is head of security here."

Willy stared at his brother. "This here's Bat Masterson's place."

"I know."

"I thought Colt said Lance was a drunk?"

"Maybe he ain't, anymore."

"We better get back to the hotel and tell him," Willy said. He flexed his hand, some of the feeling coming back.

"It ain't broke?" Danny said.

"No, it ain't, but I might wish it was by the time we tell Colt what happened here."

THIRTY-FIVE

Back inside people were slapping Lance on the back, congratulating him on the way he handled the situation. Several men were offering to buy him a drink and Lance was beginning to weaken. He was still shaking inside as the impact of what he'd done had not set in, yet. And he really could have used a drink.

He was saved by Carl Evert, who had apparently been filled in by Bat about Lance's situation.

"Get back to work, all of you," he called out, "and those of you who don't work here, get back to gambling. Sam, let me get you a cup of coffee, huh?"

"Uh, sure."

Evert put his hand on Lance's back and steered him toward a table, one of several that were kept conveniently open for the use of the staff. He called Gina over and said, "Bring two coffees, will you, honey?"

Lance sat down and laid his club on the table. His hands were shaking, and he did nothing to hide them.

"That was impressive, Sam," Evert said. "You got rid

of them without killing either of them, and without getting anyone else killed."

"I figured that was my job," Lance said. "They'll probably come back, you know."

"You're hiring tomorrow, right?"

"I hope so," Lance said, laying his hands flat on the table now in an effort to get them to stop shaking. "I don't know if the word has gotten around, though."

"I know a few boys who could use a job," Evert said. "I'll send them to talk to you. No pressure. You hire them if they seem competent enough to you."

"Obliged," Lance said. "I'll do that."

Gina brought the coffee and hurried off. Lance would rather have had a beer, or a whiskey, but he picked up the coffee and sipped it, then looked at Evert in surprise.

The pit boss smiled and said, "Gina's got instructions to always bring me my coffee with just a splash of whiskey in it. Figured it wouldn't hurt you too much."

In fact, just that one sip had quieted the shakes in Sam Lance's hands.

"Obliged again," he said, and took another sip.

"I've been where you are, Sam."

"Meaning?"

"When Bat hired me he knew that I'd been a drunk a few years ago. I managed to straighten myself out and he gave me a job. I owe him."

"How do you stay sober?"

"A little taste here and there like this helps," Evert said. "I take it a day at a time."

"How many cups of coffee a day?"

"Two, at the most," Evert said. "Sometimes none. I thought we deserved one, after this."

"I appreciate you tellin' me, Carl."

Evert put his coffee cup down and leaned his weight forward.

"Maybe I earned the right to ask a question?"

"Go ahead and ask."

"What about a gun?" Evert said. "If they come back you'll have some men behind you, but they'll have guns and you won't."

"I don't know when I'll be able to wear a gun again," Lance said. "Did Bat fill you in on what happened with Clint and me?"

Evert nodded.

"He said you managed to kill two men."

"I got lucky," Lance said, "or Clint got lucky. I killed one by accident, and one in spite of the fact that I couldn't seem to hold the gun straight."

"I understand."

"I think you do," Lance said.

"I wear a gun, but I never made my way with one, and I never . . . had an experience like you did."

"I hope you never do."

Evert raised his cup and said, "I'll drink to that."

Danny and Willy returned to the waterfront hotel in search of their brother Colton. Neither of them relished having to tell him what happened, but they didn't have much of a choice. After all, they had found Sam Lance.

They walked to Colt's room and knocked. When there was no answer they went to Zeke's door. They were about to knock when they heard the grunting and groaning from inside. Danny tried the doorknob and opened the door. What they saw was a shapely, if rather wide ass bouncing up and down on their brother Zeke. Zeke had his hands on the ass and he was the one making all the noise while the whore jumped up and down on him.

"Wanna ask him where Colt is?" Danny asked.

"Leave him alone," Willy said, still holding his injured wrist, "and close the door. It stinks in there."

Billy Drew had left the saloon with his bottle of whiskey. Colt decided to get a fresh beer and go over what he had learned. Apparently, Sam Lance was not going to be the worn-out drunk they expected to find. Also, he had somehow gotten himself involved with both Clint Adams and Bat Masterson. It looked like the four of them were going to need some help to get done what they needed to get done.

He looked around and saw that he was alone in the Wayfarer with the bartender, Tor. Zeke was probably in his room pounding that whore while Danny and Willy were gambling. At that point, while he was wondering when they might return, the two of them walked in. Willy was holding his wrist, like he'd been hurt.

"What happened to you?"

Willy sat down while Danny went to the bar, got two beers and carried them to the table.

"You ain't gonna believe it, Colt," Willy said.

Colt reached out and grabbed his brother's hand. Willy hissed, because his wrist was swollen and tender. Colt released it.

"That hand broke?"

"I don't think so," Willy said. "I can move it, just about."

"Tell me what happened."

"We went gambling at Bat Masterson's place, The Sportsman's Club," Danny said. "You'll never guess who we ran into there."

"Sam Lance."

"How'd you guess?" Willy demanded.

"Never mind," Colt said. "Lance do that to you?"

"Yeah, with some kind of club," Willy said. "He's the head of security there. We got into a . . . a tussle, and he throwed us out."

"Both of you?"

Danny nodded and Willy looked away.

"Was he wearin' a gun?"

"No," Danny said, "he just had him a club."

"He have any help?"

"No."

"Clint Adams and Bat Masterson weren't there?"

"No," Danny said, "Masterson wasn't there."

"Clint Adams?" Willy asked. "The Gunsmith? Is he in this, too?"

"Looks like it," Colt said. "So, both of you had guns, he had a club, and he threw you out?"

"Um, yeah," Willy said.

"He disarmed us," Danny said. "We didn't have a chance. He came from behind."

"He ain't the drunk you told us he was, Colt," Willy complained.

"Yeah, but he ain't wearin' a gun, either," Colt said. "At least we know where he is now."

"We gonna go and get him?" Danny asked.

"Not right now," Colt said. "If he's sober, and he's got Adams and Masterson to back him, we're gonna need help, and a lot of it. Where's your brother?"

"He's got that whore in his room," Danny said.

"Okay," Colt said, "we're gonna sit tight, your wrist is gonna heal, and I'm gonna send some telegrams tomorrow."

"The rest of the family?" Willy asked.

"That's right," Colton James said, "the rest of the family."

THIRTY-SIX

The final hand of the night came down to Clint, Tim Burroughs, and Ed Chase. Bat had folded on the third card, satisfied with the fact that he was the big winner of the game.

After four cards Clint had three sixes showing; Ed Chase had three aces; and Tim Burroughs was showing a ten, jack, queen, and king of hearts. He needed an ace of hearts for a royal flush, but Chase needed it for four aces. Clint looked at his hole card again. He made a habit of checking his hole card often, even though he always knew what it was. No one could accuse him of having a tell.

His hole card was a six. Only one of the other players could beat him, but they both needed the same card to do it.

Having played all night with Ed Chase he figured that if the man had better than three aces it was probably a full house. That would not beat him.

Burroughs was the one to worry about.

"The bet is Ed's." Bat had dealt the hand, and was sitting back and watching, at this point.

"Two hundred," Chase said.

"I call and raise five," Burroughs said, and looked at Clint.

Clint did not have the cash to play in this game, but Bat had explained that all the players were extended credit and given chips to play with. Settling up would come later, in private, with Ed Chase.

He eyed Burroughs, who would be raising if he had the ace or the nine of hearts. He could fill in on either end and win. Fortunately, Clint recalled that one of the other players had folded the nine of hearts. So Burroughs absolutely needed the ace.

With four sixes there was no way Clint could just call. He would raise, and if he lost the hand he'd have to bow to the winner and accept it. Four of a kind was four of a kind, and you had to play it.

"I'll just raise and make it an even thousand."

"That's eight hundred to you, Ed," Bat said.

Now, Chase almost never folded, so when he called it did not tell Clint anything. This man would call whether he had the ace or not. Men like Chase rarely won, but they usually had an impact on the outcome of a hand because they could not be figured.

Burroughs said, "Too late in the hand, the game, and the night to get timid. I'll raise another five hundred."

"Well," Clint said, "only one of you can possibly beat me, so I'll just call."

"Ed?" Bat asked.

Chase had stayed in the hand too long to fold now,

but to everyone's surprise he said, "I fold."

"Well," Bat said, "let's see if you have that ace, Tim."

Burroughs turned over his hole card, revealing a red ace, but it was the ace of diamonds.

"A straight," Bat said. "No straight flush, and no royal. Clint, you need better than three sixes to win this."

Clint turned over his hole card, revealing the fourth six.

"Gentlemen," Ed Chase said, "we're finished for the night."

Clint was standing off to the side with Bat, who had ended up the big winner of the night, when Tim Burroughs came over and extended his hand.

"It was a pleasure playing against you," he said to Clint. "You, too, Bat, but I was looking at this gent's face across the table all night."

"I understand," Bat said. "That was a good final hand."

Burroughs looked around to see if Ed Chase was within earshot.

"I was surprised that Ed folded after he stayed in almost every hand all night."

"Yes, I was surprised, too," Clint said.

"Shh," Bat said, as Chase approached them as the other players—all of whom had come out on the losing end of the night—filed out

"Well, since you three are the winners why don't we go to my office and I'll pay you off?"

"Suits me," Burroughs said.

"If you gents will follow me down?"

They did so, filing down the stairs and then walking through the main hall until they reached his office.

"Have a seat, gents."

The chips had been counted out at the table, so Chase knew exactly how much money was coming to each player. He chose to pay off Burroughs first, as he had the least amount of money coming.

"Thanks very much for playing," Chase said, as the two shook hands.

"Same time tomorrow night?" Burroughs asked.

"I look forward to it."

Burroughs looked at Clint and Bat. "Will you gents be here tonight?"

"Unless something comes up," Bat said.

"Should be," Clint said.

"See you then," Borroughs said, and took his leave.

Burroughs left and Chase sat down at his desk, counting out Clint's money and Bat's money from a safe behind him. Before he could pay them, though, his partner, Ed Gaylord, came in.

"Bat, you know Ed."

Bat stood and shook hands with the bigger Ed.

"Clint, my partner, Ed Gaylord."

Clint stood and shook hands.

"How'd you boys do?" Gaylord asked.

"They came out the big winners," Chase said.

"Bat was the big winner of the night," Clint said, "which is fitting, since he's the best player."

"I was just about to pay them off," Chase said.

"Don't let me stop you," Gaylord said. He refrained from asking his partner how much money he had lost.

Chase came around the desk, handed Clint a stack of cash, and Bat a larger stack. "Be happy to see you both back tonight."

"Actually," Gaylord said, before Clint or Bat could respond, "we'd be happy if you joined us in the lounge for drinks and some conversation."

"Conversation?" Clint asked.

"About anything in particular?" Bat asked.

"Well," Ed Chase said, closing the safe, "yes. It seems we have a, uh, problem we think you gents could help us with."

Clint and Bat exchanged a look.

"If you've got the time . . ." Gaylord said.

Clint gave Bat a nod and Bat said, "We'll take the time."

THIRTY-SEVEN

"We have a going concern here," Ed Gaylord said. "We're doing very well."

"I can see that," Bat said.

"We run honest games," Ed Chase said.

"That's pretty well know, Ed," Bat said. "You guys are considered square gamblers by everybody in Denver."

"Where does the problem come in?" Clint asked. "What do you need us for?"

"Bat," Ed Gaylord said, "we realize that you're the competition."

Bat waved that away and said, "Ed—both Eds—look at my place, and look at yours. I can do a good business, but I'm never gonna be a danger to you fellas. The Palace is the Palace. This is the top gaming place in Denver, bar none. I admit it."

"We appreciate that," Ed Chase said.

"Bat, we're gamblers," Gaylord said, "that's all we are. Neither of us is a gunman, and we've never worn a badge. We have a situation we don't know how to handle."

"You're getting pressure," Bat said.

"Or you're being extorted," Clint said.

The same thing had happened to Luke Short in Fort Worth with his White Elephant Saloon.

"Both," Ed Chase said. "We've been approached for protection money, and if we don't pay they're going to burn us down."

"Who is they?" Bat asked.

The two Eds exchanged a glance.

"The man who approached us was a policeman," Ed Gaylord said.

"That could be a big problem," Bat said.

"Did he actually say that your place would be burned down if you didn't pay?"

"Much of what he said was innuendo," Ed Chase said. "He said—"

"Wait," Bat said. "Were you both present when he said what he said?"

"Yes," Ed Chase said, and Gaylord nodded.

"Then you're both agreed on what was said," Clint added. "We're not going to get conflicting accounts?"

"No," Ed Chase said.

"We're agreed," Ed Gaylord said.

"Okay then," Bat said, "Tell us what was said."

Colt James went back to his room that night, concerned about what was going to happen over the next week or so. Actually, nothing was going to happen until he got his cousins to Denver. He and his brothers, backed by his cousins, were going to have to take on Sam Lance, Bat Masterson, and Clint Adams unless they could get Lance away from those other two and isolate him.

He paced the floor and looked out the window and finally decided he was giving this way too much thought tonight. He walked to the door of his room and opened it, then sat on the bed. Eventually, the bedsprings stopped squeaking in Zeke's room and his brother stopped grunting and groaning. When he heard the door to Zeke's room open he got up and stepped into the hall. The blonde whore turned and looked at him.

"You done there?" he asked.

She was more than done. In spite of the fact that Zeke smelled, he was better in bed than his older brother—or, anyway, he could last longer. She'd been with him a few hours and she felt like she'd been plowed for a week.

"Yeah, I'm done. Why?"

"I'm in need of a little company."

She was tired, but she knew this one wouldn't last long, and eventually he'd drift off to sleep and she could do the same.

"Why not?" she asked. "I'm here."

She entered his room and he closed the door behind them.

"We were told," Ed Chase said, "or warned, that accidents can happen."

"Accidents like fire," Gaylord added.

"And he told us that we could probably use a little extra protection for the Palace."

"Do you have protection now?" Clint asked.

"We employ some men to be bouncers. But—"

"No security?" Bat asked.

"Not formally."

"You need security," Bat said. "Hire somebody to be the head, and let him hire men to work under him. That's what I've just done."

The two Eds exchanged another look.

"What?" Bat asked.

"We were kind of hoping you'd give us a little more than advice," Ed Chase said.

"You want us to step in?" Clint asked.

"We'd pay you—" Ed Gaylord said.

"I don't hire out my gun, Ed," Bat said.

"Neither do I."

"We just thought," Ed Gaylord said, "that since you're in the same business as we are—"

"Do you know of any other saloons or gambling houses who are paying this kind of protection?" Bat asked.

"No," Ed Chase said.

"I'll tell you what," Bat said. "Since we're in the same business why don't we contact some of the other gambling-hall and saloon owners and see if they're paying. Maybe we can all join forces and put a stop to this extortion."

"Have you been approached, Bat?" Gaylord asked.

"No," Bat said, "but I haven't been open all that long."

The two Eds looked at each other.

"What do you think?" Chase asked.

"It's worth a try," Gaylord said. "If these men are making their living this way then they've approached more than just our place."

Chase looked at Bat.

"So you'll work with us on this?"

"Sure," Bat said. "As colleagues. No money changes hands."

"Done," Gaylord said. He stepped forward to shake hands, and then Ed Chase did the same.

"And what about you, Mr. Adams?" Chase asked.

"I'm just along for the ride," Clint said. "I'll back Bat's play, whatever he says."

"Excellent!" Gaylord said happily.

"I'll get back to you tomorrow afternoon," Bat said, "but until then, would you mind telling us the name of the policeman who approached you?"

"Sure," Gaylord said, "it was Stoker, a Lieutenant Stoker."

THIRTY-EIGHT

It was late when Clint and Bat got back to The Sportsman's Club. During the ride back they discussed the problems of the two Eds, and the fact that they knew the policeman who was apparently fronting for an extortion racket.

"Wonder if there's a Longhaired Jim Courtwright behind this, like that time in Fort Worth?" Bat said.

"Somebody's got to be behind it," Clint said. "Stoker can't be running the play, and fronting for it at the same time."

"He's a smooth talker," Bat said. "He plays at the club a lot, but never for big money."

"Maybe he's just taking a look at your operation before making his pitch," Clint suggested.

"He makes his pitch to me, innuendo or not, I'll pitch him out on his ear."

When they entered the club they found Carl Evert there, apparently waiting.

"Carl," Bat said. "Problems?"

"Maybe," Evert said.

"Do we need to talk in private?"

"No," Evert said, "I'd say this concerns Mr. Adams, as well."

"Well then, let's go into the office. Have somebody lock up for us, huh?"

"I'll take care of it," Evert said. "Meet you in there."

"What do you think is on his mind?" Clint asked.

"I guess we'll find out in a few minutes."

Bat had poured three brandies by the time Carl Evert arrived. Clint was already seated holding his, so Bat handed Evert his when he entered.

"How'd you fellas do at the game?"

"We did okay," Bat said. "How did things go here?"

"They were . . . interesting." He went on to explain how Sam Lance had handled the situation with the two brothers.

"Wait a minute," Clint said. "You pulled Lance into a situation like that and he hadn't even started the job?"

"We were crowded," Evert said, "packed. I knew something was going to happen and I wasn't sure how to handle it without gunplay. I just thought Lance would have something to suggest."

"But he handled it instead," Bat said.

"Right," Evert said, "and you should have seen the way he handled it."

"How was he afterward?" Clint asked.

"Kind of shaky," Evert said. "I had Gina bring him some coffee. There were plenty of people offering to buy him a drink."

"Wait a minute," Bat said. "You had her bring coffee?"

"Yes."

"For both of you?"

"That's right."

Bat leaned forward.

"One of your coffees?"

"Well . . . yeah."

"His coffees?"

"With a shot of whiskey in it," Bat said.

Evert looked at Clint.

"It's the only way I can have whiskey," the man explained. "I used to be a drunk."

"Did the coffee help Sam?"

"Yes," Evert said. "His hands stopped shaking and he felt better."

Bat looked at Clint.

"Looks like my security man handled the situation."

"I guess," Clint said, "but what about the two men? Think they'll be coming back?"

"Maybe," Evert said. "Sam seemed to think so."

"He's going to hire some help tomorrow, right?" Bat asked.

"I have some men coming in to interview," Evert said.

"Good men?"

"That'll be up to Sam, I guess."

"I'll have to put the word out, too," Bat said. "We've got to put a team together before those two men do."

"That'll be up to Sam, too, won't it?"

"Yes," Bat said, "It will. I'll talk to him in the morning. You did the right thing, Carl. It worked this time."

"Thanks." Evert finished his brandy and set the glass down on Bat's desk. "Good night. See you both in the morning."

After Evert left Bat said, "Sounds like your boy Sam did okay, today."

"He's your boy, now."

"Yeah, I guess."

"Let's see how he feels after he thinks it over tonight," Clint said. "He needs to get through the night without a drink, and hopefully without bad dreams."

"We all have bad dreams."

"Not the kind he has," Clint said. He stood up and set his glass down next to Evert's. "I've got to get some sleep."

"Yeah, me, too."

They left the office together and Bat walked Clint to the front door to let him out.

"Gonna play tomorrow night?" Bat asked.

"Sure, why not?"

"What are you gonna do tomorrow during the day?"

"I don't know. I thought I might see if Tal Roper was in town. I meant to stop in on him before now, but . . ."

"You got busy with other things."

"Yeah."

"Okay."

"Why? You want me here in the morning?"

"For breakfast?"

"Why?"

Bat shrugged and said, "Just in case."

Clint took a deep breath.

"Look, I know he's my employee now, more my responsibility than yours, but I just thought it might help if you were here when he, you know, comes down."

"Yeah, okay," Clint said. "Seems like there's a lot of favors being done here back and forth."

"Ain't that what bein' friends is all about?"

"Sure seems that way," Clint said. He gave Bat a little punch on the shoulder. "Good night, Bat."

" 'Night, Clint."

Bat watched Clint walk away, then backed up, closed the doors, and locked them behind him.

THIRTY-NINE

Clint woke the next morning thinking about Sam Lance, wondering what kind of night he had. He also wondered how much more involved he wanted to be with Lance, but now that the man was involved with Bat, he didn't seem to have much choice.

On the other hand, the way he handled the situation the night before in The Sportsman's Club was impressive—especially for a man who only a couple of days before was a full-fledged drunk.

He dressed, tried to decide where to have breakfast, then remembered he'd promised Bat he'd eat at the Sportsman. With him. And Sam Lance.

Sam Lance woke with a start, sitting straight up in bed. He was covered with sweat, and his sheets were soaked. He sat that way for a while, trying to recall the dream he'd been having, but he couldn't. Usually, when awoke this way he knew what he was dreaming—usually that he was holding Dulcy in his arms when she died. But this morning he couldn't recall the dream at all.

He considered that a huge step forward.

Colt James woke with a telegram in his mind. He was going to send it to all his cousins, and to some of his friends. All he had to do was find a telegraph office.

Willy James woke with a painfully swollen right wrist and hand. He wished he had drawn his gun much quicker last night and blown a hole in Sam Lance.

Danny James awoke wondering what was wrong with betting a dollar on a hand of blackjack. A dollar was a lot of money to him. Wasn't it a lot of money to everyone?

Zeke James awoke thinking about the blonde whore and whether or not he should get her back to his room tonight. She really didn't seem to mind the smell that his brothers said he had—not that he ever noticed it, himself.

Daphne Gibbs woke up that morning wondering if she had done the right thing by Sam Lance. She was also a little confused about her feelings for him. Did she have any, or was she simply doing this for Dulcy? And how was she going to feel now that Bat Masterson had hired Sam, and he was going to be around all the time, reminding her of Dulcy?

•   •   •

When Bat Masterson awoke he was mostly satisfied with his life. Business was good, his kitchen was greatly improved, he'd won a lot of money last night, his old friend Clint Adams was in town, and his new security man seemed to be good at his job. And now he was going to talk with some of the other sportsmen in town to see what they could do about Lieutenant Stoker and his extortion racket. And in doing this, perhaps he would move to the forefront of the business world here in Denver.

He got dressed, checked himself in the mirror, and did not leave his room until he was sure he looked impeccable. He hoped that, at breakfast, he and Clint would discover a new and changed Sam Lance, and that the man would be willing and able to get on with his job. If that was the case then Bat would have a private security force in place by the end of the week. Having his kitchen problems and security problems solved in the same week was more than he could have hoped for.

He went downstairs to have breakfast with Clint and Sam Lance.

FORTY

Bat saw Daphne when he came downstairs. She was on her way to the dining room for breakfast because she'd heard about the new cook and wanted to try the food.

"Can you do me a favor, first?" Bat asked.

"Of course."

"Would you ask Sam to meet me and Clint in the dining room for breakfast, too?"

"All right. What time?"

"As soon as he can," Bat said. "I expect Clint any minute."

Daphne nodded and went off to deliver the message. Bat was surprised at how young and fresh she seemed with her face devoid of all the saloon-girl paint she wore while working.

As Bat entered the dining room he saw Clint Adams coming in from the other direction.

Clint saw Bat, who waved him over. Bat also maintained a table of his own in the dining room—one he would be getting more use out of since hiring Sandy as his cook.

"You remembered," Bat said.

"Just barely," Clint said. "How about Sam?"

"I sent Daphne to get him," Bat said. "I just hope he hasn't changed his mind about the job—not after his performance yesterday."

"Bat, what do you want to do about Stoker?" Clint asked. "I mean, after all, he is a policeman."

"I've been thinking about that," Bat admitted. "I was wondering if maybe we couldn't find out something about him, something he wouldn't want anyone to know, that we could use against him."

"And how do you expect to do that?"

"Well," Bat said, "you were hoping to see Talbot Roper today, and he is the best private detective in the country. I'm sure he has all kinds of contacts in Denver."

"So you want me to ask Roper to help?"

"Not as a favor," Bat said. "As you pointed out yesterday, there's too many favors floating around as it is. Tell him he'll be hired."

"By who? By you?"

"No, by the coalition."

"What coalition."

"The one I'm going to form of all the owners of gambling establishments or saloons in Denver."

"You have been thinking about this."

"Just a little."

By the time Sam Lance joined them they had a pot of coffee on the table, and three cups. As soon as Bat saw

Lance coming toward them he poured the man a cup.

"Thanks," Lance said, sitting down, "I could use one of these."

"Heard you had some excitement last night," Bat said. "Heard you handled it about as right as anyone could."

"I did all right," Lance said, lowering his cup. "I'm more excited about what happened to me after that."

"What happened?"

"I woke up this morning from a bad dream."

"And was that unusual?" Bat asked.

"No," Lance said, "what's unusual is that I usually—I always remember what I dreamt about. This morning I couldn't remember at all."

Studying Lance now Clint thought the man looked better than at any time he had seen him over the past few days.

"You look good, Sam," he said.

"I feel good."

"So you're still ready for this job?" Bat asked.

"More than ready. I'm going to be doing interviews today."

"Think your bad boys from last night will come back?" Bat asked.

"If they do it will be with help," Lance said, "so the sooner I can hire some men the better."

"Sam," Bat said, "some friends of mine are having a problem."

"What kind of problem?"

"Security."

"Another gambling house?"

"The biggest gambling house in the city," Bat said.

"The Palace. They're going to be needing some security."

"But I work for you," Lance said.

"I don't want you to work for them," Bat said. "I was thinking I'd . . . loan you to them. Let you look over their operation and make some suggestions. That sort of thing."

"I could do that."

"You should know that there's some extortion going on," Bat said, "and that Clint and I intend to stop it."

"Well, you can count on me to help any way I can."

"I appreciate that," Bat said. "For now let's just have our breakfast and get our day started. I think we're all going to be pretty damn busy today."

FORTY-ONE

Clint's first stop after leaving The Sportsman's Club was Talbot Roper's office, to see if he was even in town. As he entered he saw that Roper had yet another young secretary.

"Do you have an appointment?" the pretty young red-head asked.

"No," Clint said. "I'm not a client, I'm a friend of his."

"What's your name?"

"Clint Adams."

At that her head jerked up and she stared at him.

"Really?"

"Yes."

"You're him?" she asked. "I mean, he told me that he knew you, but you're really him, aren't you?"

"I'm Clint Adams."

"The Gunsmith," she said, "you're really him."

"Is Tal here? Is he in town?"

"Oh, I'm sorry," she said. "Yes, he's here. I'll just tell him . . . you're him, really?"

"Yes, really."

"I'll just tell him . . . just wait here, okay?"

"Okay."

She went through the door into Roper's office after a short knock, and then reappeared.

"You can go in."

"Thank you."

He slid past her into the office. Roper, a big, handsome man, was sitting behind his desk, but he came out from behind it to shake hands with his friend.

"Why didn't you let me know you were coming?" Roper asked. "I might have been away."

"It was sort of spur of the moment, Tal," Clint said.

"It's good to see you. What brings you here?"

"The Sportsman's Club. Have you been there?"

"Masterson's place," Roper said, sitting on the edge of his desk. "No, I haven't."

"How about the Palace?"

"Haven't been there, either."

"Well," Clint said, "I've sort of backed into an offer for you, if you're free to hear it."

"I'm always free to listen, but let's go someplace else to talk."

He grabbed his hat and jacket, told his secretary he'd be back shortly, and then led the way down the street to a café.

"Too early to start drinking," he told Clint, as they were seated.

"I understand."

"My secretary is very impressed with you," Roper

said. "She came into my office saying, 'It's him, it's really him.'"

"She must be easily impressed."

"No, I talk about you all the time," Roper said. "I keep trying to impress my secretaries with the fact that I know you, but they just keep getting impressed with you."

A waitress came over and they ordered coffee.

"Okay, so this isn't just a friendly visit," Roper said. "What's on your mind?"

"It was supposed to be a friendly visit but, like I said, I backed into this. Tal, do you know a policeman named Stoker?"

"Lieutenant Wayne Stoker," Roper said. "Sure, I know him."

"Wayne?" Clint asked. "I didn't know his first name."

"How did you meet him?"

"Well, there's a story behind it," Clint said, and went on to tell Roper about Daphne Gibbs; Sam Lance; Kingdom, Colorado; and a Denver waterfront alley.

"That is an involved story," Roper said. "Stoker was on the docks, huh?"

"Is that where he usually works?"

"Stoker's kind of special, Clint," Roper said. "He works wherever he wants to."

"How did he earn that kind of freedom?"

"I'm not sure," Roper said, "but I think it's what, and who, he knows."

"He was pretty interested in Sam Lance the other day, and now I find out he's involved in an extortion racket."

"He's got his fingers in a lot of pies."

"Bat and I don't know how far this extortion thing spreads, but we'd like to stop it before it goes much further."

"So what do you need from me?"

"It's like what you said about Stoker," Clint replied. "Who he knows, and what he knows. I think we need to know a little something about Lieutenant Stoker."

"And you want me to find out?"

"Who's got better contacts in this city than you?"

Roper thought a moment, then said, "I'll see what I can do. I might know somebody with some information. I'll need to pay for it, though."

"You submit a bill to Bat, and you'll get paid."

"As long as it's not coming out of your pocket."

"I'm not a partner here, Tal," Clint said. "I've got no vested interested beyond doing a favor for Bat."

"And for the girl, Daphne, and for Sam Lance, from what I can understand."

"It's like Bat says," Clint commented. "There are too many favors going around."

FORTY-TWO

Colt James had to leave the waterfront to find a telegraph office, and he found himself uncomfortable wandering the streets of Denver. The city was just too big for his liking. He was glad he left his brothers at the hotel. They would have been like little children, either fascinated, or scared to death.

When he located the telegraph office he sent two very short telegrams, not wanting to spend too much money to get them sent. When his family members got it, they'd know what to do.

"You want to wait for the answers, sir?" the clerk asked.

Colt thought he should wait, otherwise the replies might never get to him in that waterfront hotel. Besides, it was a pretty safe bet that most of them would answer right away.

"I'll wait for the answers," Colt said. He peered out the window and saw a saloon across the street. "I'll be over there. Can you bring them over when they come in?"

"I'll have to wait for more than one at a time," the clerk said. "Can't leave the office for one telegram."

"That's okay," Colt said. "I'd rather get them two or three at a time, anyway."

The clerk shrugged and watched through the window as Colt walked across the street and entered the saloon.

By mid-afternoon Sam Lance had hired four men to be part of The Sportsman's Club's security force. He had instructions from Bat to hire ten men. It was up to Lance to schedule where and when they would work. He had already decided to have half of them on duty in the gambling hall during the busiest hours of the night. He'd keep two on during the day, and rotate them all from day to day, so that the two who worked days Monday would work nights on Tuesday. Two of the five who worked Monday night would have Tuesday off. Only one man would ever end up working three nights in a row. And he, himself, would be on duty most nights.

He had finished his interviews for the day. He'd done them at a table toward the front of the hall, one that was farthest away from the bar. As he was getting ready to leave, Daphne came over and sat down.

"Can we talk a minute?" she asked.

"Sure, Daphne," Lance said. "What can I do for you?"

She studied him for a moment. His face still had a pasty, unhealthy look, but his eyes were clearer. She thought that if he could stop drinking and put on some weight he'd start to look good.

"I just wanted to say—or to ask—now that you're

working here, do you think there'll be a problem—I mean . . ."

"What kind of problem?" he asked. When she didn't answer right away he said, "Do you mean, with us reminding each other of Dulcy?"

Daphne pushed her hair away from her face and said, "Yes, I suppose that's what I mean."

"Well," Lance said, "I can tell you that I would never need to see you to be reminded of my wife, Daphne. I think about her every day. What about you? Is this gonna be a problem for you?"

"Well, I don't think about her every day," she said, "but I loved her. She was my best friend, and I think about her a lot. I—I've never had another woman friend since she died. Not one that I was close to."

"Does that mean there will, or won't be a problem?"

She hesitated, then said, "No, of course there won't be. That would be silly. I'm glad you got this job, and I'm glad you've stopped drinking, Sam."

"Well," he said, "I don't know yet if I've actually stopped. It'll probably be some time before I know for sure."

"Well, you're trying," she said. "That's important. I'll see you later. I have to go and do some shopping."

"Okay," he said, "see you tonight."

Daphne left and Lance sat there for a short time, so that by the time he was ready to leave again Clint walked in and stopped him.

Clint entered The Sportsman's Club through one of its two entrances. The first entrance put you in the main hall, while the second brought you right into the gaming hall and saloon. When he walked in he saw Sam Lance preparing to leave a table—a table which was as far from the bar as you could get.

He walked over and intercepted him.

"How'd the hiring go?" Clint asked.

"Oh, hey," Lance said. "It went fine. I hired four men. Three of the four had been sent by Carl."

"How many men did you interview?"

"A dozen."

"Not bad for the first day. What was wrong with the other eight?"

"Too young, too cocky, too good to take orders from an old drunk . . . that sort of thing."

"That kind of talk's not going to help anything."

"Yeah, I know," Lance said. "One of them recognized me, said he thought I was dead drunk—or dead."

"Well, you didn't hire him, did you?"

"Actually, I did. He struck me as competent."

They both laughed at that.

"Have you seen Bat around?"

"No," Lance said, "not lately. Might be in his office. I've got to go. I checked with Bat and he said we could afford to outfit our men with guns. I want them all carrying the same reliable weapon."

"Good idea."

"I'm gonna go and look at some now." He started away, then stopped and turned to Clint. "Want to come along?"

Actually, Clint would have, since he was an expert on guns, but he decided to let Lance do it alone.

"No, that's okay," Clint said. "I've got to see Bat about a few things. I'll see you later, though."

"Sure," Lance said, then added, "thanks." The thanks was for Clint knowing that Lance was perfectly capable of picking out reliable weapons himself.

Sam Lance went out the front door and Clint went up to the bar, where two bartenders he hadn't met yet were working.

"Anybody seen Bat?" he asked.

One of the young men looked up and said, "I think Mr. Masterson's in his office."

"Thanks."

He walked past them, and no one tried to stop him. Not good security, at all. He'd have to tell Lance about that.

FORTY-THREE

Clint knocked on Bat's door and entered. His friend was seated behind his desk, obviously going over the books.

"Come on in and have a seat," Bat said. "I'm just going over some figures."

"Hope you're doing well," Clint said. "I just talked to Sam. Sounds like you're going to commit a lot of money to security."

"Ten men, outfitted the way Sam wants them," Bat said. "I think I can afford that."

Clint sat and waited for Bat to finish what he was doing and close the books.

"Did you see Roper?" Bat asked.

"I did, and he's on the job. I told him to bill you."

"Fine."

"Have you talked with other owners yet?"

"Several, all smaller than me, and certainly smaller than the Palace. None of them have been approached by Stoker, and they're a little leery of committing money to stopping something that hasn't started yet."

"They never heard of paying for prevention?"

Bat frowned. "That sounds just like what Stoker's selling."

"Whoa," Clint said, taken aback by his own words, "it does."

"Well, I'll keep talking to them, and to others," Bat said. "I can't believe that the Palace is the only place they've approached."

"What if they're not only hitting gambling halls and saloons?" Clint asked. "What if they're going after other business, like maybe the bigger hotels?"

"I didn't think of that," Bat said. "I'll have to check."

"By the way, nobody tried to stop me from walking back here," Clint said. "I'd talk to Sam about that if I was you."

"I did," Bat said. "He's going to put two men on duty during the day. Once it starts getting busy in the evening, we'll go to five."

"Sounds like a good plan."

"I think he might work out, Clint."

"I hope so," Clint said, "but I'd expect him to slide back a time or two. You might have to be patient, Bat."

"I'm a very patient man," Bat said. "It's an attribute that serves me well at the poker table. Speaking of which, you want to get some dinner before the game?"

"Sure," Clint said, "but I'm not ready to eat, yet."

"Neither am I. Two hours, in the dining room?"

"I'll meet you there."

"I've still got some books to go over, so get out."

"See you later."

Bat opened some more books and Clint took his leave.

• • •

For Colt James it had been a good morning and after-noon. Within a couple of days he and his brothers would be joined by a dozen men, mostly cousins, some friends, all good with guns. Their whole family was always good with guns, that's why it had been such a shock five years ago when Steve was gunned down by Sam Lance.

Colt went back to the hotel to tell his brothers what had happened, and to check on Willy's wrist. He found both Danny and Willy in their rooms. From Zeke's room came the sounds of bedsprings and grunting and groan-ing. Between him and Zeke they were gonna wear that poor whore out. He wondered if she was the only one who worked this hotel. Maybe she had a deal with the desk clerk.

He knocked on the door and Danny answered it.

"How's Willy's wrist?"

"Come on in," Danny said.

Colt entered and saw Willy sitting by the window.

"Willy?"

His brother scowled. "Still can't hold a gun, Colt. I wanna kill that Lance!"

"You'll get your chance," Colt said. "Del and Joe, Adam and Ross, and eight others will be here within the next couple of days. When they get here we'll go and burn down that club around Sam Lance's ears."

"What about Masterson, and Adams?" Danny said. "They ain't just gonna sit by and watch."

"We'll take care of them, too," Colt said. "There'll be enough of us to do it."

They fell silent for a moment and the only sound was of Zeke's bedsprings. The three of them exchanged a glance and then Colt said, "I'm gonna go downstairs and see if that clerk knows any more whores."

Wayne Stoker rolled the body over and looked down at Billy Drew. The old drunk had finally gotten hold of a real bad bottle of whiskey, and it had killed him.

"Take him away," he told his men.

He had better things to concern himself with than dead drunks. Sam Lance had disappeared on him, but Clint Adams was still at the Denver House. And it was almost time for him to go and talk to Bat Masterson about accidents that could happen to a place like The Sportsman's Club. In fact, he decided right there and then that today was the day to try to sell Bat some insurance.

FORTY-FOUR

Clint met Bat for dinner and they had another marvelous meal prepared by Sandy. Word seemed to have already gotten out because the place was three quarters full rather than half.

"Won't be long before this place is full every night," Bat said, after they'd finished eating.

"You might end up having to give her a raise."

"We'll see about that," Bat said. "She might even be worth it. Come on, I'm supposed to go and meet some of my new security men before they go on duty for the night."

They left the dining room, walked across the main hall and into the gaming hall and saloon. Lined up there, waiting with Sam Lance, were five men wearing the same color shirt and trousers, and wearing the same Colt in their holsters—the same holsters. Two of them were also holding shotguns.

"Uniforms," Clint said.

"In this kind of place a show of power is a deterrent," Bat said.

"You still might think of having a man or two blend into the background."

"I'll see what my new head of security thinks of the idea."

When they reached the row of men Sam Lance said, "Here are your first five, Bat."

Bat looked at the men, all practically standing at attention, and said, "Jesus, I hope you're not running this like a military operation, are you, Sam? I mean, they don't have to stand at attention and call you Captain, do they?"

"No," Lance said, "they're all just real impressed to be working for you."

"You men," Bat said, "I'm Bat Masterson. I answer to Bat. Don't call me Boss. That's Sam. Got it?"

They all nodded and some of them said yes.

"This is Clint Adams. He's a friend of mine and will be around for a while. He can go wherever I can go, so don't shoot him. Understood?"

They all laughed and nodded that they understood. Clint noticed that on the other sides of their gunbelts they were wearing billy clubs like Lance was carrying. There was a hole in the top, where a leather thing was strung through.

"Okay, then, go to work and keep my place and especially my customers safe."

"Let's go, boys," Lance said, and led the way.

"All ages and sizes," Clint said. "I saw one fella who looked about twenty-five and another who looked fifty-five, one real skinny and kind of bulky."

"Sam didn't play any favorites," Bat said. "That's good. You ready to go and play poker?"

"I'm ready."

They turned to leave and as they almost reached the main hall they both saw Lieutenant Stoker walk in.

"Well, well," Bat said.

"Do we want to avoid him and go to the game, or do we want to hear what he has to say?"

Bat scratched his nose for a moment, then said, "The game will still be there. Why don't we hear what he has to say?"

"If he's going to make his pitch to you," Clint said, "he'll want to talk to you alone."

"I got no problem with you hearing his pitch," Bat said.

"Why don't we play it this way?" Clint asked. "You talk to him alone. Let's not let him know how far on the inside of this thing I am. We might want an edge later. What do you think?"

"I think it sounds like a sound strategy. Why don't you stay here and we'll even let him approach me alone?"

"Good idea," Clint said. "I'll wait for you in the saloon."

"Gambling hall and saloon," Bat said.

"Excuse me, I stand corrected," Clint said. "I'll see you in the gambling hall."

Bat stepped out into the main hall, where Stoker could not miss seeing him.

FORTY-FIVE

"Have a seat," Bat said when he and Stoker entered his office.

"I hope I didn't catch you on your way," the lieutenant said.

"Actually, you did," Bat said, "but that's okay, we can talk." He seated himself behind his desk while the policeman sat directly across from him. "What's on your mind?"

"Well, Bat—can I call you Bat?"

"I thought we already established that the other day," Bat said. "And I'll call you . . . Lieutenant."

"Actually, I'm not here as a policeman."

"Really? What are you here as?"

"A friend, really," Stoker said. "You see, I know that you're already doing very well, Bat, for not having been open even a month."

"I've been lucky," Bat said. "People in Denver like to drink, and gamble."

"Yes, they do," Stoker said, "but people who gamble tend to be emotional, as well."

"I have always found that an emotional gambler is a bad gambler, Lieutenant."

"I agree," Stoker said, "but it's the emotional gamblers who are also the bad losers, and bad losers . . . well, there's never any telling what they might do."

"In my experience," Bat said, "bad losers usually come back to pour good money after bad. It's the kind of thing that would keep someone like me in business."

"I'm sure you're right, Bat," Stoker said. "After all, you are very experienced as a gambler."

"I am."

"So running a place like this without insurance of some kind . . . well, that would be the huge kind of gamble a man like you would appreciate, wouldn't it?"

"Insurance? I'm not sure what you mean," Bat lied, knowing that the pitch was coming.

"I'm talking about the bad gambler who walks out the door and returns later to toss a fiery torch through the window."

"Ouch," Bat said, "that is a bad gambler."

"See, if you had someone who could keep an eye on him, make sure he didn't get to toss that torch—"

"You're talking about security!" Bat said, as if he had just realized it. "Private security."

"Well," Stoker said, "we prefer to think of it as insurance—"

"We? Who is we?"

"The people I work with who supply the service."

"So you do this in addition to your police work."

Stoker spread his hands. "Police work does not pay all that much, Bat."

"Oh, I know it," Bat said. "I've worn a badge a time or two in my day."

"Yes, you have," Stoker said, "but with us on board you wouldn't have to worry about security."

"Well . . . I don't think so, Lieutenant."

"Let me make my offer perfectly clear, Bat."

"Please do."

"We would offer you all the protection you need against fire, theft, or anything else that might . . . put you out of business."

Bat leaned forward.

"Let me be very clear, Lieutenant."

"Please do."

"What you are talking about is not insurance, it's not even security, it's protection. You want to sell me protection."

"Well . . . if you want to put it that way."

"And there's another way I could put it, too."

"And what way would that be?"

"Extortion."

"Extortion?" Stoker said. He laughed. "You haven't even heard my offer. The cost would be minimal, considering how well—"

"The cost is going to be nothing, Lieutenant," Bat said, "because I'm not going along with this. And by the way, neither is the Palace."

"The Palace?"

"Yes," Bat said. "I believe you're also waiting for an answer from Ed Chase and Ed Gaylord."

Stoker scratched a space just above his right eyebrow.

"They, uh, spoke to you about this?"

"Oh, yes," Bat said, "they did. And I can give you their answer right along with my answer. Nobody is paying."

Stoker sat silently for a moment, cleaning some non-existent dust from his trousers with swipes of one hand.

"Bat," he said, slowly, "I don't think that would be advisable."

"Why not?"

"Well, I'm very aware of your reputation, but that rep was earned, oh, shall we say in the Wild West atmosphere. I mean, Dodge City, Tombstone, those days are surely gone. This is Denver. This is a big city. You're out of your element in a big city. Why don't you let us assure you of the safety of your place, your people . . . your livelihood."

"Dodge City," Bat said, "Tombstone, my time in those towns gave me experience in dealing with vermin, *Mister* Stoker, and that's what you are . . . vermin. Also, the people you either work for, or with. You're all vermin, and big city or not, I can handle vermin."

"Bat—"

"Let me warn you," Bat said. "I have my own security force, Stoker, and my own head of security. Within the next few days the Palace will have the same. These will be our own private little police forces, so I'd think twice if I was you about coming back here or going back to the Palace with your offers, or your threats."

"Threats? I haven't made any threats."

"That's because I didn't give you a chance to," Bat said. "I have somewhere to go and I couldn't wait for you to beat around the bush. I really wish that you people with your protection rackets would speak plain English, for once."

"Bat, you're making a mistake—"

"Stoker," Bat said, "I don't know what your connections are, or how high up they go. If I went to the Commissioner of Police with your actions here today I'm sure you would be able to squirm your way out of trouble, so I'm not going to bother. If you or any of your people come around here looking for trouble, my security chief and I will handle it on our own."

"And your security chief, would that be Clint Adams?"

"Clint is my friend, but he is not in business with me and he is not employed by me. My security chief is Marshal Sam Lance."

"Lance?" Stoker laughed. "You hired that drunk as your head of security? You are in need of protection, Bat."

Bat stood up, which caused Stoker to come to his feet quickly.

"Get out, and don't come back to my place, Stoker. Not as a man, not as a policeman, and not as the vermin you are."

"Big mistake, Bat," Stoker said, moving carefully toward the door, "big mistake."

"My biggest mistake," Bat said, "is probably letting you out of this room alive."

Stoker went out the door very quickly, before Bat had time to change his mind.

FORTY-SIX

During the cab ride to the Palace Bat told Clint about his conversation with Stoker.

"I know what you're going to say," he ended. "I jumped the gun a bit with the news about the security for the Palace and all, but he was taking too long to get to the damned point."

"And this after you told me what a patient man you were."

"Never mind," Bat said. "Maybe I convinced him to stay a policeman and leave extortion to the professionals."

"Or maybe now you not only have to worry about those two coming back from the other night with Sam, but somebody coming back on behalf of Stoker. After all, you don't have any idea who's behind him, or how many men they have at their disposal."

"I'm not worried," Bat said. "My new security force can handle anything."

"You've got a lot of faith in some men you've just met—and some of whom you haven't met yet—and a

229

security chief who only a few days ago was a drunk."

"Now you sound like Stoker—again."

"No, this time I'm being realistic. I just wish Sam had time to settle into the job before he was challenged."

"Well, he rose to the challenge the other night."

"One night, one incident, two men," Clint said. "Can't judge him off of that."

"I'll keep a close eye on him," Bat said. "If he falters hopefully there will be someone under his command to take his place until I can hire someone else."

"Under his command?" Clint asked. "Now who's thinking of this in military terms?"

"I tell you what," Bat said, as they came within sight of the majestic Palace, "I'm going to stop thinking about this now and start thinking about poker."

"Now you're talking."

As it turned out they weren't late at all for the game. The only problem was that nine men appeared for the game, down from twelve the night before. They solved the problem the same way. They all sat at one table and played five card stud. By the halfway point of the game, after one fifteen minute break, they were down to five players—Bat, Clint, Tim Burroughs, Ed Chase, and the politician, Andrew Harris. Once again most of the money was in front of Bat, Clint, and Burroughs. Harris had managed to play even while there were more players in the game, but quickly started losing when the game got down to five. Chase was barely in the game when the sixth man left, and was the first of the final five to drop. He remained to watch, and to officiate in the event of a dispute.

"Let's break one more time," Chase suggested at one point, and they all agreed.

"This'll probably be the only way I'll last a little longer," Harris said, rising. "It surely is a pleasure playing with men who know the game."

"Thank you, Andrew," Chase said, as if he was included in the thank-you when they all knew Harris was speaking of Clint and Bat and possibly Tim Burroughs.

Chase had brought a girl in to take drink orders and she did so now. When she returned, her tray was laden with full beer mugs.

"Nothing like a good cold beer this time of night," Harris said. He was a big, florid-faced man whose face got even redder still when he drank. He was partial to three-piece suits, and wore a gold watch chain and fob that he fiddled with on occasion.

"I thought you were an early-to-bed type when you weren't gambling, Andrew," Chase said.

"Well, there are times when my colleagues and I go this late into the night hashing out a bill, Ed."

"What have you been hashing out these days, Andrew?" Bat asked. The two had fallen into a first-name basis on the first night.

"Well, Bat," the man said, "I'm afraid there are some of my colleagues who would like to see gambling outlawed."

"No!" Chase said, appalled.

"Imagine if that happened, Ed," Bat said. "You and I would be reduced to mere drink peddlers."

"Don't even joke about that!" Chase said.

"Don't worry, Ed," Harris said. "I'm managing to hold them off, but there are those who believe that gambling simply leads to additional outlets for criminal activity."

"What kind of criminal activity?" Chase asked, as if the very idea were preposterous.

"Well, extortion, for one. Protection rackets. That sort of thing."

Chase fell silent but tossed a look both Clint and Bat's way.

"People don't only extort gambling halls, Andrew," Bat said. "I'm sure there are those who try to sell protection to large hotels, big business, as well as to gamblers."

"I hope that none of that is happening in our fair city, Bat," Harris said. "At least, that's the position I'm taking when the question rears its ugly head."

"That there is no protection racket in Denver?" Bat asked.

"None," Harris said. "If there was I would know about it. I'm the leading law-and-order man in this state."

"That's right," Bat said, thoughtfully, "you are, aren't you?"

"So, if anyone was trying to run that kind of action in Denver you'd know about it?" Clint asked.

"Without a doubt."

As the men turned to return to the game, Clint leaned over to Bat and asked, "What is he, a congressman?"

"Senator."

"Are you thinking what I'm thinking?"

"I'm thinking about asking some questions," Bat said, "what are you thinking?"

"I'm thinking about having Talbot Roper ask some questions."

"Ooh, that's better thinking than what I'm thinking," Bat said. "Let's do that."

"You fellas comin' back to the game?" Senator Andrew Harris—the leading proponent of law and order in the state of Colorado—asked.

"We're coming," Clint said. To Bat he whispered, "Wouldn't the leading law-and-order man be against gambling?"

"One would think," Bat said, "wouldn't one?"

FORTY-SEVEN

This time the final hand came down to Clint, Bat, and Burroughs. The reason was obvious: they were the only ones left in the game. Andrew Harris had dropped out only two hands after that last break. He bid all the players good night and good luck.

"I hope he's playing with his own money," Burroughs commented after Harris left, "and not his constituents'."

"Remember," Chase said, "he's the leading law-and-order man in the state."

"I do remember," Burroughs said. "I'm glad I'm just passing through."

The setup on the last hand was this: After three cards Bat had an incredible three aces. Why stay in the game, except that Burroughs was once again building a straight flush and possible royal flush—this time in spades. He had the ten, jack and king showing.

Clint had two eights showing and a third one in the hole. He'd been lucky last time, and lucky all night. It was time to see if his luck would hold on the last hand.

Burroughs had dealt the hand so he said, "It's Bat's bet."

"Five hundred."

Obviously, this was going to be a big pot.

"Call," Burroughs said, which meant he was willing to wait and see if he would catch the fifth card in his straight-royal flush.

Clint's plan was to make Burroughs fold or pay through the nose to wait for his card.

"Raise a thousand," he said. It was a foolish bet. He was beat on the table by Bat's three aces. If no one improved Bat would win. If it had been earlier in the game Clint would never have made the bet, but as it was the last hand and he was well ahead—again—he figured, why the hell not?

"I'll call and make you wait to pay," Bat said.

They both looked at Burroughs, wondering if that last card was worth a thousand to him.

And it was.

"I call."

Burroughs's dealt out the fifth card to each player. Clint caught a card that enabled him to fill up, giving him a full house, eights over threes. Bat did not improve on the table, catching a deuce, but if he had a deuce in the hole then he had filled aces over deuces. If he had an ace in the hole he was going to be hard to beat. But Burroughs caught the nine of spades. So he now needed the Queen to fill his straight flush.

Clint had played in many games where the last hand was decided by a pair of three, or something similar. Now, in two nights, they were looking at potential hands of four of a kind or a straight flush—and he was sitting on possibly the low hand of the three.

"Bat's high on the table," Burroughs said. "Three of a kind to my four card flush to Clint's two pair."

Bat said, "A thousand," without hesitation.

Burroughs hesitated just long enough for both Bat and Clint to know he hadn't filled his hand. He also realized that his hesitation had cost him any chance of bluffing and said, "I fold," disgusted with himself.

But Clint knew one thing from Burroughs's play. The nine had not helped him, so he had needed the queen or an ace. If he needed the ace, then Bat didn't have four of them. However, Bat could still have a higher full house than he did.

Clint knew that Bat could be playing his cards, or he could be bluffing, and very few men could have read him. They had been friends for so long that Clint could often read Bat's bluff. In this instance, however, he could not, so he paid to see the card.

"I call."

"Aces full," Bat said, flipping over his hole card, another deuce.

"Beats my full boat," Clint said. "Congratulations, Bat."

"And gentlemen," Ed Chase said, "that is the game. If you will come downstairs with me we'll settle up in my office, and then I would like to buy you each a drink in the lounge."

They all went downstairs.

Chase paid them off in his office, Bat being the big winner, then Burroughs, and then Clint.

"That hesitation at the end," Burroughs confided to Clint on the way down the stairs, "that cost me."

"It cost you a chance to try and bluff," Clint said, "but it didn't cost you the hand. You were beat by both full houses. In all probability one of us would have paid to see your card, and maybe both."

After they were paid off they went with Chase to the lounge for a last brandy.

"I don't know if I'll have enough players for a private game tomorrow night," Chase said. "I could send a message to each of you if I do. I know where to contact Bat."

"I'm at the Denver House," Burroughs said.

"So am I," Clint said.

"I'm surprised we haven't crossed paths in the dining room or the bar," Burroughs said.

"I'm afraid I've only made it down to the dining room for breakfast," Clint said.

"Clint's been taking most of his meals at my place."

"Yes, I heard you had a new cook," Chase said.

"The word is out already?" Bat asked, secretly pleased.

"Oh yes," Chase said, "seems your kitchen rivals ours now."

"Well," Bat said, "I'll never rival your gambling layout, Ed, so allow me the small victories."

"Hmm," Chase said, "I'm thinking I may need a new cook fairly soon."

"You should know by now, Bat," Clint said, "that there are no small victories. That would imply that there are small losses, as well."

FORTY-EIGHT

The first night with Sam Lance's security force in place went smoothly. Clint found that out when he had breakfast with Bat again. After breakfast he went to Talbot Roper's office to take up the question of Andrew Harris with the detective.

"I know how you hate coincidence, Clint, but maybe this isn't one," Roper said, from behind his desk.

"Have you got something on Stoker, already?"

"Stoker is Harris's boy."

"You're right," Clint said, "that may not be such a coincidence. What else?"

"Plain and simple," Roper said, "I believe that if Stoker is working a protection racket, he's doing it for Harris."

"The top law-and-order guy in the state is a criminal?"

"Who better?" Roper asked. "Who's going to question him, and if push comes to shove, who's going to arrest him?"

"A Federal Marshal, that's who."

"All you've got to do is come up with some evidence."

"Oh, no," Clint said, "I'm not getting involved in cleaning up Colorado's politics. All I'm doing is helping Bat. And by the way, Bat's already listened to Stoker's pitch and sent him packing."

"Well, if they're serious about working this game," Roper said, "they'll try to make some kind of example of Bat's place. Fire seems most likely. It can always be passed off as an accident."

"Bat's still building up his security force, but I'll talk to Sam Lance about this."

"How is Lance working out?"

"So far, so good, but it's really still too soon to tell," Clint said. "When things get hairy, that's when we'll see what he's got left."

"I hope he comes through," Roper said. "He's been through a lot. You want this report on Stoker?"

"Yes," Clint said, reaching for the folder, "and whatever you can get on Harris."

"Harris will have wiped his shoes clean before entering the state house," Roper said. "My feeling is he wants to be governor."

"So he can loot the state?"

"Possibly."

"Damn!" Clint swore. He knew himself better than anyone. He was not going to be able to walk away from this and let a crooked politician become governor.

"You can't get to Harris, Clint," Roper said, "if that's what you're thinking."

"What do you suggest?" Clint asked.

"Well," the detective said, "the next best thing would be to cut off his right arm. You're just going to have to find a way to do it."

"I get the feeling that if we just wait," Clint said, "he'll come to us."

FORTY-NINE

Over the next couple of days Clint talked with Bat and with Sam Lance about Lieutenant Wayne Stoker and Senator Andrew Harris. Lance finished hiring his men and now had a full force of a dozen. He'd originally intended to hire ten, but Bat told him to add two more. They were going to have to be ready for anything Stoker could throw at them. With this in mind Lance had even hired a man with experience fighting fires.

The next few days were busy for the James Brothers as well.

Colt James made it clear to the hotel clerk that he wanted to take over the hotel. The clerk said he'd have to check with the manager, but Colt told him not to worry about it.

"Every room will be filled," he said, "and ain't that what your manager wants?"

"Yes, but . . . some of the rooms are already occupied."

"Un-occupy them!" Colt told him. "My men will be

tired when they get here and I don't want them to have
to wait for rooms. Is this all clear to you?"

"Clear," the clerk stammered, "v-very clear, sir."

Colt James instructed his brothers Willy and Danny to
rent buggies so they could ferry their cousins and friends
from the train station to the hotel. He asked Willy about
his wrist, to which his brother replied, "Still can't pull
the trigger on a gun, but I think I can handle the reins
of a buggy."

"Good," Colt said. "I want you and Danny to drive
everybody here. I don't want Zeke at the station."

Zeke was fascinated by trains, and one time he had
wandered onto the tracks to get a closer look at an on-
coming train and had almost gotten himself killed.

"What's he gonna be doing?" Danny asked.

"I'm gonna let him keep playing with his whore," Colt
said. "It'll keep him occupied and out of trouble."

So Danny and Willy drove back and forth to meet
every train, and in two days time all twelve of the men
Colt had contacted were occupying rooms in the hotel.
The clerk had managed to evict the people already occupying some of the rooms, and he'd done it just in time.

"You did good," Colt told him, and handed him ten
dollars. "Now just keep doing what I tell you and we'll
get along fine—and you might even make some money."

Colt needed someplace to meet with his men so he could
talk to them all at one time, and he chose the Wayfarer
Saloon. He told Tor much the same thing he had told
the clerk in the hotel.

"You're closed for business except to me and my men," he said.

"I gotta eat—" Tor started to complain.

"Don't worry," Colt said. "My family and my friends like to drink and eat. You'll have plenty of business."

The look in Colt's eyes told Tor he would brook no argument, so the Wayfarer owner finally agreed.

On the night of the third day after he sent out his telegram Colt and his brothers Willy, Danny, and Zeke met with six of their cousins, and six of Colt's friends and compadres at the Wayfarer Saloon to plan their strategy for getting their revenge on Marshal Sam Lance.

"Danny and Willy have already seen Lance at The Sportsman's Club," Colt told them. "What we need to do is have somebody he don't know and has never seen to go in there tonight and get some idea of what we might be up against. Is Lance handling security himself, or has he hired help? That kind of thing."

"Colt," Jerry James, a cousin, said, "I don't think one man would be handlin' security for the whole place."

"Why not?" Paul Kane asked. He had ridden with Colt a time or two, and had always made money, which was why he was in Denver. "Bat Masterson's the owner, right? That means you gotta deal with Lance and Masterson."

"And Clint Adams," Colt reminded him.

"How much more security they need?" Kane asked.

"A lot," Colt said, "because they're gonna have to deal with us. We got sixteen men. Let's find out what they got. Who wants to go in?"

"I'll go in," Kane said. "I wanna get a look at Masterson and Adams, anyway."

"Okay," Colt said, "one more."

"I'll go with him," Jerry said. "A family member should be there. After all, this is about Steve, isn't it?"

"And money," Kane said. "Somebody said something about money."

"Oh, there'll be money," Colt said. "See, I figure while we're in there takin' care of Sam Lance, we might as well rob the place, too."

"Rob Bat Masterson's place?" Cousin Ralph James said. "That would make us damned famous!"

"Then that's what we'll be, Cousin," Colt said, "good and goddamned famous."

FIFTY

"Come on in, Sam," Bat said. "Have a seat."

Sam Lance entered Bat's office and took the only empty chair. Clint Adams was sitting in the other one.

"Hello, Clint," Lance said.

"Sam."

Lance looked at Bat and asked, "What's up, Boss?"

"Have we got all our men in place?" Bat asked.

"All twelve of them know their shifts."

"We might have some trouble heading our way, Sam," Bat said.

"We've talked about this, Bat," Lance said. "Fire, some kind of accident."

"I think we should be ready for more than that," Bat said. "I think we should be ready for any kind of a frontal assault."

"You mean a robbery?" Lance asked.

"Maybe that, too. Clint has some ideas I'd like you to listen to," Bat said.

Lance turned his gaze on Clint.

"First of all, I'm not second-guessing you at all, Sam,"

Clint said. "You're in charge of your men. I just have an idea or two—"

"You don't have to explain, Clint," Lance said, cutting him off. "I know your reputation. If you have something to say, just say it."

"Okay," Clint said. "We're dealing with a man— Lieutenant Wayne Stoker—who has friends in high places. He's got protection, so he might think that he can get away with almost anything."

"I understand that."

"I'm thinking that sometime in the next couple of days he's going to send somebody in to take a look at your security. If that happens, you don't want them to see everything you've got."

"You're telling me to put some men in regular clothes and let them blend in," Lance said, "then when they see the uniformed men we have posted, they'll think they've seen it all."

"Exactly."

Lance shrugged and looked at Bat. "Makes sense to me, Bat."

"Good. Any sign of those two boys who caused trouble your first night?"

"Not yet, but I cracked one of them a good one on the wrist. My bet is they'll wait till he heals to come back, and they'll bring help."

"How do you like that?" Bat asked. "We got to watch out for two groups of men. What a pain in the ass it would be if they all decided to hit us at one time."

"We can handle it, Bat," Lance said. "I haven't known

these men very long, but I interviewed them and I trust them all."

"Plus you've got Clint and me," Bat said. "Press us into service at any time."

"I appreciate that, Bat," Lance said. "After all, it is your place. You're the boss."

"That may be," Bat said, "but security is your responsibility. Just have your boys keep their eyes open for anybody who's not gambling, drinking, or chasing the girls."

"I'll alert them."

"Okay," Bat said. "Thanks for coming in, Sam."

"That's it?"

"That's all."

Lance got up, waved to both of them and left the office.

"What do you think?" Bat asked.

"Clear-eyed and his hands are steady," Clint said. "So far so good."

"Clint, I have a request."

"What's that?"

"We're going to get hit," Bat said. "That seems inevitable."

"I agree."

"I'd like you to move here from the Denver House, just until this all blows over. I need you here."

"Say no more, Bat," Clint said. "I'll go and get my gear and move in right away."

"Thanks," Bat said, "I appreciate that."

Clint stood up and started for the door.

"There's one other thing," Bat said.

"What's that?"

"You mentioned a drunk, a little guy on the waterfront who was friends with Sam?"

"Billy Drew," Clint said. "Haven't seen him since we got Sam to stop drinking. Why?"

Bat picked up a newspaper and said, "He's dead. Says here he was found in an alley, the victim of some bad whiskey."

"That's too bad," Clint said, "but not surprising."

"I'm wondering if Sam read about this."

"He hasn't mentioned it."

"Just how friendly were they?"

"How friendly are two drunks sharing a bottle, Bat?" Clint asked. "Once they sober up they probably forget about each other."

"You're probably right," Bat said. "I just don't want anything pushing Sam over the edge again."

"I'll try and find the right moment to bring it up," Clint said. "That is what you're asking me, isn't it?"

"You know," Bat said, "I'm gonna start arguing more strenuously with people when they talk about how dumb you are."

"I appreciate that, Bat," Clint said. "I really do."

FIFTY-ONE

Jerry James walked into The Sportsman's Club in the company of Paul Kane.

"Remember," Kane said. "Play something, blackjack, roulette, anything, but don't just stand around gawking. You know what Lance looks like?"

"I got a description," Jerry said.

"I saw him once," Kane said. "I'll point him out. Let's go to the bar first."

They walked to the bar and ordered a beer each. Kane used the bar mirror to examine the room. Immediately, he saw two security man. They were wearing a sort of uniform, sidearm, and a billy club. He tried to see more, but that was all he could use the mirror for.

"Let's split up," Kane said. "See if you can count the security men. This is their busiest time. Let's see how many men they have working."

"Right."

"Buy some chips to carry around."

"Okay."

They split up, each carrying their beer. At a different table they each bought some chips. True to his family name, Jerry James bought one-dollar chips. As he walked around, every so often he stopped at the roulette wheel and put one down. The first time his number came in he got so excited he forgot about counting security men.

Paul Kane was more professional. He'd ridden with both Steve and Colt James. He knew that other than them the rest of the family was pretty stupid. Not as dumb as Zeke, maybe, but not particularly smart. He had been glad to see some of the boys Colt had brought in other than his family. He'd ridden with both Digger Williams and Abe Dominick before, and knew what they were capable of.

Kane found a seat at the end of a blackjack table and played halfheartedly. By the time his chips were gone he had counted six uniformed security men.

Now he wondered how many were there that weren't in uniform.

Kane had seen Sam Lance before and would recognize him. He saw him there, did not count him as one of the six security men. What Kane failed to realize was that he was better known than he thought. The minute Sam Lance saw him, he recognized him.

Lance found his way to Bat's table, where Bat and Clint were seated. Clint had already collected his things from the Denver House and had moved in upstairs.

"Does the name Paul Kane sound familiar to either of you?" he asked.

"No," Bat said, and Clint shook his head.

"He rode with Steve James."

"The man you killed in Kingdom?" Bat asked.

"That's right," Lance said. "He's also ridden with Colt James, Steve's brother."

"And Kane is here?" Clint asked.

Lance nodded.

"He came in with another man, probably looking the place over."

"Why would he—" Bat asked, but Lance cut him off excitedly.

"I knew there was something familiar about those two men the other night, and now there's something familiar about the man with Kane."

"What is it?" Bat asked.

"They look alike."

"So?"

"They also looked like Steve James."

That took a moment to sink in, and then Bat said, "You're saying that Steve James's brothers are in Denver?"

"I've probably seen three of them now, and Paul Kane—and if Kane's here I'm betting Colt James is too."

"Sam," Clint asked, "just how big a family did Steve James have?"

"There's four brothers . . ." Lance said.

"That's not too bad," Bat said.

". . . and a shitload of cousins. They also have friends

like Paul Kane who have ridden with them. Bat . . . they were looking for me the other night."

"Well, they found you, and you handled them."

"They've been trackin' me for years," Lance went on, "only I never cared much about it."

"And you do now?" Bat asked.

"Look," Lance said, "you've got enough trouble with Stoker and whatever trouble he's gonna pull. You don't need me here attracting the likes of these James brothers and their kin."

"You're not walking out on your job now, are you, Sam?" Bat asked.

"Bat, I just don't want you to pay too high a price for hirin' me."

"Why don't you let me worry about that?" Bat said. "Meanwhile, why don't you get back to work?"

"Maybe I should have a talk with Kane," Lance suggested.

"No," Clint said, "ignore him. Don't let on that you recognized him."

"And then what?"

"Maybe he'll go back to these James brothers and tell them to forget it. You're too well insulated here, Sam, with all your security."

"I don't think they'll give up, Clint," Lance said. "Steve was their older brother."

Clint looked at Bat. "You up to some night crawling?"

"You want to follow these two yahoos back to their lair?" Bat asked.

"Might as well find out where they're holed up. We might even find out how many there are. After all, they sent someone to check us out. Least we could do is return the favor."

"You've got a good point," Bat said. "Sam, point out Paul Kane to us, and then you can get back to work."

"Sounds like I'm going to miss some fun," Lance said.

"Oh, we're just going to take a look," Bat said. "Shouldn't be any fun to miss, at all."

Lieutenant Stoker watched from across the street as Clint Adams and Bat Masterson left The Sportsman's Club. They looked as if they were following someone, but that was of no concern to him. All he had to do was give them enough time to get far enough away before he made his move.

This was going to be easier than he'd thought.

FIFTY-TWO

"We're taking a chance leaving Sam alone with Stoker out there," Clint said.

"We've got a chance to clean this all up, Clint," Bat said. "We can take care of Sam's problem while he takes care of mine. I have faith in him, Clint."

They followed the two men—Paul Kane and a member of the James family, according to Lance—until they reached a buggy they had left a few blocks from the club.

"Uh-oh," Bat said. "I'm not up to running after them, are you?"

"No," Clint said, "but if the James family came here looking for Sam Lance they must have gotten the word that he was here."

"So?"

"So, Lance was down on the waterfront until we took him away from all that."

"You think these clowns are heading for the water-front?"

257

"One way to find out," Clint said. "Let's go back to the club and get a cab."

"I'm with you," Bat said.

When Stoker was sure the coast was clear he broke from his cover, crossed the street and entered The Sportsman's Club.

As they approached the club they both saw a man crossing the street and heading for the door.

"You see what I see?" Bat asked.

"That's Stoker."

"Now what do we do?" Bat asked.

"Head for the waterfront and let Sam handle it, I guess."

Bat hesitated.

"You did say you have faith in him."

"I did say that, didn't I?"

"What are you two whispering about?"

They both turned quickly, each feeling annoyed that someone had been able to creep up on them like that. However, when they saw who it was they both relaxed.

"You look like you're plotting something," Talbot Roper said.

"What are you doing here?" Clint asked.

"I followed Stoker," Roper said. "Just wanted to see what his day was like. He ended up here. He was hiding across the street in a doorway after you fellas left. Guess he thought it was safe to go ahead into your club, Bat."

"Is he alone?" Clint asked. "Have anybody with him?"

"Not that I could see."

"What's he planning?" Clint asked.

"That I don't know."

"But nobody's with him?"

"Not unless he put some people inside ahead of time."

"We'll have to let Sam handle it," Bat said.

"So where are you fellas headed?"

"The waterfront," Clint said.

"What for?"

"A little fun," Bat said. "You up for a little fun, Roper?"

"Fun's my middle name, Bat."

"Come on," Clint said, "there's a cab in front of your place now. Let's grab it."

As the three of them ran over to stop the cab before the driver could drive off Bat said, "Fun ain't a name. What kind of middle name is that?"

"What kind of name is 'Bat'?" Roper asked.

"Ouch," Clint said. "He's got you there, Bat."

"Never mind," Bat Masterson said. "Let's just get in that cab . . . *Talbot*. What kind of name is Talbot?"

FIFTY-THREE

On the way to the waterfront Tal Roper gave Clint and Bat the rundown on the place.

"The place for all the drunks and thieves to congregate is the Wayfarer Saloon."

"I've been there," Clint said. "Charming place."

"The other saloons on the Front are either too small, or too clean, if you can believe it. They also don't stay open as late as the Wayfarer."

"What if they're in a hotel?" Bat asked.

"I'm sure they are staying in a hotel," Roper said, "but there are only a few down there. They're fleabags with no bars or dining rooms. If this James family is having a meeting on the waterfront, the Wayfarer is the place."

"Let's check it out," Clint suggested. "If Tal is wrong then we just keep looking."

"Suits me," Bat said.

Roper leaned forward and gave the driver instructions to take them about a block from the Wayfarer Saloon.

"On the waterfront?" the driver called back, looking frightened.

"Don't worry," Roper said. "I'll protect you, and double your fare."

"Okay," Roper said, staring down the street at the well-lit Wayfarer Saloon, "we can all march down there together, or I can slip down and have a look."

"Go ahead and slip," Bat said. "We'll wait here."

Roper nodded and faded into the shadows.

"He as good as they say he is?" Bat asked.

"Better."

"Can he handle a gun?"

"Real well."

"Trust him with your back?"

Clint looked at Bat. "I trust three men above all others with my back, Bat. You're one of them, Jim West is the second, and Talbot Roper is the third."

"What about Wyatt? And Luke?"

"Okay," Clint said, "they're fourth and fifth—but I'm trying to make a point."

"I know, I know," Bat said, "I get it. I'm just givin' you a hard time."

"You worried about what's going on back at your place?"

"Yes."

"Having second thoughts about leaving it to Sam?"

"No," Bat said, "I just wish I was there to see it."

"Maybe we'll finish up here in time to go back and catch the action."

Before Bat could reply Roper was back.

"Sixteen."

"What?" Bat asked.

"There are sixteen men inside. I recognize two of them. Paul Kane, and Digger Williams."

"I know that name," Bat said, "Digger."

"There are posters out on both of them," Roper said, "and rewards."

"When did you turn bounty hunter?" Bat asked.

"Hey," Roper said, "they're in there, and there's a reward for them. Do the math. Besides, if I collect the rewards I won't bother billing you for my services."

"Hey," Bat said, "be my guest. The reward is yours."

"Sixteen?" Clint repeated.

"I counted twice," Roper said. "That doesn't count the bartender. The place seems to be closed down for them."

"How many doors in and out of that place?" Clint asked.

"Two, front and back."

Clint looked at Bat. "Sixteen."

"Ah," Bat said, "they're outnumbered."

"We could use some shotguns," Clint said.

"I bet they've got shotguns in there," Bat said.

"They do," Roper said.

"Think they'd mind if we borrowed them?" Bat asked.

"I don't think we should give them a chance to refuse."

"Okay," Clint said, "Two front, one back. How's that?"

"Who gets the front?" Bat asked.

"I think Clint should go in the front," Roper said.

"Why Clint?" Bat asked.

"Because he's the Gunsmith," Roper said. "He'll scare 'em more."

"Yeah," Bat said, looking at Clint with a grin, "you're the Gunsmith. Scary."

"You guys are scary," Clint said. "Okay, I'll go in the front, but you better be ready to come in the back and cover me."

"Hey," Bat said, "we'll cover your back."

"The doors are flimsy," Roper said. "One kick opens 'em both."

"How many guns you got?" Bat asked Roper.

"Two. A Peacemaker, and a short-barreled Colt. Cut it down myself so it fits—"

"Give Clint the Peacemaker. He should have both hands full when he walks in."

"Good idea," Clint said. "Hand over the Peacemaker."

Roper tugged the longer-barreled gun from his belt and handed it to Clint.

"Okay," Clint said, "five minutes enough?"

"Plenty," Roper said.

"Good luck," Bat said. "Don't miss."

"He won't miss," Roper said to Bat. "He's the Gunsmith."

"Don't call me that!" Clint said to their backs.

"Yeah," Bat said to Roper, "don't call him that . . . *Tal.*"

"What kind of name *is* Bat?" Clint heard Roper reply. "You still haven't told . . ."

FIFTY-FOUR

The joking was over.

Clint stood outside the front door of the Wayfarer. He could hear the sounds of the men inside talking. This could have been any kind of a meeting, perhaps even one of the Waterfront Merchant's Society, but the fact that Roper had seen and recognized Paul Kane made it clear that these were the men they wanted. Clint wanted to be dead sure of that because the shooting was bound to start as soon as he entered, or soon after. He felt if he could get a few words in first, maybe he could avoid bloodshed.

He palmed his own gun in his right hand, Tal Roper's Peacemaker in his left.

Five minutes were up!

Roper kicked the back door and it didn't budge.

"Wha—" he said.

"You said the doors were flimsy."

"They used to be," Roper said. "They must have reinforced them. Come on, kick with me."

"Clint's probably in there already!" Bat said.

"Then kick!"

They both kicked, and the door not only opened, it splintered.

Colt James heard the front door slam open and saw Clint Adams step inside, a gun in each hand.

"Clint Adams!" Paul Kane shouted, and instead of galvanizing the men into action, it froze them—except for Digger Williams, who went for his gun. Clint shot him in the chest before he could clear leather, and Digger fell to the floor.

"That's the Gunsmith, Colt?" Zeke James asked, anxiously.

"That's him, little brother."

Suddenly, they heard the sound of the back door splintering and both Bat Masterson and Talbot Roper came rushing in.

"Masterson," Kane said to Colt in a very conversational tone.

"Who's the other one?" Colt asked.

"Don't know."

"I'll introduce him," Clint said, "and maybe I should do most of the talking."

"Why's that?" Colt James asked.

"Because we have the drop on you."

"Maybe the question should be . . . why?"

Bat saw a shotgun leaning against a table to his left. He made a quick grab for it and held it one-handed. He felt better.

"Hey," Zeke yelled, "that's mine!"

"Zeke!" Colt shouted.

If his stupid brother made a move toward Masterson he'd be dead in seconds.

"Zeke, no!" Danny threw his arms around Zeke and restrained him.

"But that's mine. Colt gave it to me."

"Forget it," Danny said, holding his smelly brother tightly.

"You ain't fair, mister!" Zeke shouted at Bat.

"If that's your brother, then shut him up, Colt," Clint said. "You are Colt, aren't you?"

"I am," Colt said, "and you're crazy. You come barging in here, shooting up the place, killing one of my friends—"

"Shut up, Colt," Clint said. "All of you, whatever you have planned for Sam Lance and The Sportsman's Club has been called off. I suggest you all go home."

Someone started laughing. Clint looked and saw that it was Colt.

"You're facing fifteen men, Adams," he said, "and there's three of you."

"There was sixteen of you to start," Clint said. "Want to try for fourteen?"

"Come on, step up!" Bat shouted. "Who wants to be next?"

"I didn't sign on to face no Gunsmith and Bat Masterson," one man said.

"We was supposed to be facing some washed-up old drunken has-been," another man said. "Not this."

"Good decision, boys," Clint said. "Why don't the

two of you drop your guns and that'll set an example for the rest."

"Nobody drop your guns!" Colt shouted. "If you do they'll shoot you, anyway."

"Anybody who drops his gun can walk out the door and keep going," Clint said. "Oh, by the way, the other man with Bat? That's Talbot Roper. Ring a bell?"

"That's it," the first man said, hearing Roper's name tossed into the mix now, "I'm done. Here's my gun." He dropped it to the floor.

"Mine, too," the other man said, and dropped his.

"Step past me boys and keep going," Clint told them. "Don't make the mistake of stopping."

Both men eased past Clint and practically ran out the door. Two more followed, dropping their guns to the floor.

What remained was James brothers and cousins and Paul Kane. Eleven men.

"Eleven to three odds, Colt," Clint said. "Go for your guns anytime."

"Steady, boys," Colt said. "We go for our guns you'll gun us down for sure. If we leave, we can come back again."

"Wrong," Bat said. "Don't ever come back again, Colt. Next time we won't do any talking."

"Give me my shotgun!" Zeke shouted, and grabbed the barrel. That made Bat's finger pull the trigger and a full serving of buckshot nearly cut Zeke James in half.

"Damn it!" Willy James said. He went to draw his gun but his wrist hurt so much he could do nothing with it when he got it out of his holster. Of course, Roper didn't know that, and shot him.

Guns were drawn, and everybody was committed to the battle.

FIFTY-FIVE

The key to surviving a gun battle is to keep your head. Clint, Bat, and Roper all knew that. Most of the James family did not. They all started yanking their guns from their holsters or pants, bringing their shotguns to bear, pulling triggers way too fast and too soon without aiming. Meanwhile, Clint, Bat, and Roper squeezed off shots methodically, and despite the fact that they were outnumbered three to one, when the dust settled they were still standing, unbowed, unscathed—and out of bullets.

They all did the professional thing and reloaded quickly before moving among the bodies to check and make sure they were all dead.

"You wanted to talk them out of this, didn't you?" Bat asked.

"I wanted to give them a chance," Clint said.

"You did," Roper said. "The smart ones left. This bunch would have been dead sooner or later, anyway, if not here tonight—and violently. These types never die in bed."

The three men exchanged glances that said they knew
that they were also the type of men who didn't die in
bed.

They heard some movement behind the bar and all
three turned, guns pointed, to see the bartender standing
there, uneasy.

"Don't shoot!" he said, throwing his hands up. "They
made me close up for them to have their meetings."

"Where were they staying?" Clint asked.

"Fleabag hotel a few blocks away. I understand they
took that over, too."

Clint looked down at the bodies. He could see what
Sam Lance had meant about the resemblance. He walked
over to Colt James, leaned over him and made sure he
was dead.

"Is anyone missing?" he asked the bartender. "Other
than the men who walked out, and these men here, is
there anyone else?"

"I don't know—"

"Take a look!"

The man came out from behind the bar and prowled
about the bodies, examining them very quickly.

"I—I don't think so. I think they're all here."

"Looks like Sam's trouble with the James family is
finished," Bat said.

"We should get back to the club and see if your particular problem has been handled, as well."

"I doubt Stoker went in just to gamble. I told him he
wasn't welcome."

"We should also wait here for the police."

"I'll wait for the police," Roper said. "You two go on back."

"Don't try to keep our names out of it," Clint said. "That'll only get you in trouble. Tell them we'll come in tomorrow and make statements."

"Fine," Roper said. "It's bound to be somebody I know. I'll handle it."

Bat reached out and shook Roper's hand. "Thanks."

"Any time . . . Bat."

When they left the saloon they went in search of a cab.

"I have a bad feeling," Bat said.

"We'll be back soon," Clint assured him.

They found a cab and gave him the address of The Sportsman's Club. As they were drawing near Bat was steeling himself in case they saw a glow on the horizon, like something burning. Clint could feel the tension in Bat.

"You really do have a bad feeling."

"Just came over me at the saloon," Bat said. "Like a feeling of impending doom."

"Sam can handle everything, Bat," Clint said. "It'll be okay. You'll see."

"Yeah," Bat said, "maybe. It's just that . . . I can see my master plan going up in smoke."

"Hey," Clint said, "Stoker and his boys could burn the Palace down instead of your place. That would also ruin your master plan."

"Oh great," Bat said, closing his eyes. "Thanks. I hadn't thought of that."

FIFTY-SIX

When they reached The Sportsman's Club the street was filled with people who had obviously fled from it.

"I knew it!" Bat said, jumping down from the cab. He started running toward the entrance to the gambling hall and saloon.

Clint hurried after him. There was no sign of fire, and he didn't smell any smoke, but there was no telling what might have happened inside to force all the people out. And they weren't leaving. The die-hard gamblers were milling about, hoping that they'd be allowed back in to continue their play.

As Clint entered he saw Bat standing in front of Sam Lance who, despite a gash on his head, was speaking very calmly. Off to one side Bat's staff of bartenders, saloon girls, and dealers looked on. Clint saw Daphne looking very concerned, but she took the time to wave to him, and he waved back.

". . . really handled the whole thing very well," he was telling Bat as Clint reached them.

Bat turned to Clint. "That sonofabitch Stoker tried to burn the place down."

"What happened?" Clint asked Lance.

"He came in and said he wanted to question me. Said he was still doing an investigation into the shooting we had in the alley the other night."

"Trying to occupy you."

"Yes," Lance said. "While I was talking to him apparently some of his men came in through the hall. My boys spotted them right away. They started a shoving match with some customers and my boys closed it. No guns, just clubs. That's how I got this." He indicated the cut on his head.

"More misdirection."

"Yep," Lance said. "While all this was going on he apparently had a man who forced a back door, entered and tried to start a fire."

"I knew it!" Bat said, again. He was seething, as if someone had abused a child of his.

"Frank Parks, the guy I hired who used to be a firefighter? He took care of it. He and two more of my boys closed in on the guy, but not before he started a small blaze. They took care of him while Parks put the fire out. We cleared the people out just in case."

"Where are Stoker and his men?" Clint asked.

"The police have them," Lance said.

"Stoker, too?"

"They took him with them," Lance said, "but I don't know if they arrested him. After all, he didn't do anything tonight."

"Maybe his men will talk and implicate him," Bat said.

"And maybe not," Clint said. "It's more than likely they never spoke to him, that he hired them through someone else. I think you know two things after this, Bat."

"What's that?"

"You're going to have to deal with Stoker as long as he's got the senator behind him."

"Guess I might have to take an interest in politics. What's the second thing?"

Clint looked at Sam Lance and said, "Looks like you hired the right man."

"I guess so," Bat said, patting Sam on the back. "Get that cut on your head looked at."

"Okay."

"And have some of your boys herd my customers back in—the ones who stuck around, anyway. Let's get them to gambling again."

"Right, Boss."

"By the way," Clint said, as Lance started past him, "your trouble with any of Steve James's family is over."

"What do you mean?"

"They're all dead."

"All of them?"

"Brothers and cousins. Some of their friends didn't like the odds and took off."

Clint walked to the door with Lance, filling him in on what happened.

"It wasn't the way I wanted it to end," Clint said, "but they didn't give us a choice."

"You and Bat did that for me? Faced down that whole family?"

"Well, we had help from one other friend, a man named Talbot Roper."

."Amazing," Lance said, shaking his head, as if to dispel a fog. "How do I deserve such good friends?"

"It all started with Daphne," Clint said. "Maybe you should talk to her."

Lance grabbed one of his men who was going by and said, "Start letting the people back in."

"Okay, Boss."

Lance looked at Clint.

"Maybe you and Daphne can—"

"Daphne was Dulcy's friend," Lance said. "To tell you the truth, I never liked her and she never liked me. We put up with each other for her sake."

"I didn't get that impression."

"Actually, I think we're friends now—but as far as a companion, I'm looking more toward Sandy, right now."

"Hey, that's great," Clint said. "Sandy's a nice woman."

"Very nice, and close to my age. Look, I've got to get to work. We'll talk tomorrow."

"Okay."

Clint turned and saw Daphne walking toward him. He realized he'd been keeping her at arm's length, unsure of what her relationship with Lance had been, or would be.

He didn't have to worry about that, anymore.

FIFTY-SEVEN

Clint remained a guest of The Sportsman's Club for several more days. During that time Sam Lance had gone over to the Palace and helped them put together a security force. Lieutenant Stoker had not been arrested and still remained free to work his protection racket for Senator Andrew Harris. He did not, however, return to The Sportsman's Club while Clint was still there.

Clint decided to leave Denver. Dealing with the crooked police and politicians of the city were the problems of Bat Masterson, Talbot Roper, and the two Eds who owned the Palace. He'd wanted to visit with Bat, see his new place, and play some poker. He'd done all that. Time to move on.

He woke the morning he was going to leave with Daphne crouched over him. She was kissing his neck and his chest, brushing his skin with the bare nipples of her breasts.

"Didn't take long to wake you, I see," she murmured.

"How could I sleep with you pressed up against me?"

He reached for her, drew up onto him and kissed her. He slid his hands down to cup her ass, then flipped her over so abruptly that she cried out in surprise.

"I'm hungry," he said.

"Well, we can have breakfast—"

"Not for breakfast."

He kissed her breasts, bit her nipples, then worked his way down her body until he reached the object of her hunger. He lifted her legs so that they were straight up in the air, then spread them and held them there so that she was completely open to him. He proceeded to devour her avidly, licking and sucking her, his face wet from her, feeling her legs begin to tremble as she cried out, pressing herself to his mouth, gasping for breath and finally exploding beneath him, bucking wildly as he continued at her, not letting up until she fell silent and still, totally spent.

It was his way of saying good-bye.

Downstairs he had a farewell breakfast with Bat, who then walked him to the door.

"This master plan of yours," Clint said to Bat.

"Buying the Palace? What about it?"

"You really think you're going to be able to put in two years here, in one place?"

"Oh sure," Bat said. "My wandering days are over. I like it here."

Clint eyed him dubiously.

"I mean it, Clint."

Clint shook Bat's hand warmly and said, "I know you mean it, my friend . . . now."

EPILOGUE

In 1888 the two Eds, Chase and Gaylord, let it be known that The Palace Theater could be had for a price. Bat Masterson met that price and he renamed the place The Palace Variety Theater and Gambling Parlors. It was the premier gambling palace in the West. He met Emma Walter, who performed a song-and-dance number there, and later married her. Bat owned and operated the theater for only a couple of years, and then sold it and moved on.

**Explore the exciting Old West with one
of the men who made it wild!**

JAKE LOGAN
TODAY'S HOTTEST ACTION WESTERN!